A MOODY FELLOW FINDS LOVE AND THEN DIES

A NOVEL BY

DOUGLAS WATSON

Outpost19 | San Francisco
outpost19.com

Watson, Douglas
        A Moody Fellow Finds Love And Then Dies
        / Douglas Watson
        ISBN 9781937402624 (pbk)
        ISBN 9781937402631 (ebook)

Library of Congress Control Number: 2014900600

OUTPOST
19

PROVOCATIVE READING
SAN FRANCISCO
NEW YORK
OUTPOST19.COM

Also by
Douglas Watson

The Era of Not Quite: Stories

For Michelle

Everyone gets to die. Not everyone gets to find love first.

Some people don't even get to look.

This novel is about a moody fellow who got to do all three. His name was Moody Fellow.

Moody looked for love for a long time before he found it. He looked in some, not all, of the wrong places and in quite a few of the wrong ways. It didn't make things any easier that, from the beginning of his search to the short-lived sweetness that marked its end, he was a terribly—and we do mean awfully—moody fellow.

But enough ado. Let us begin at the beginning.

2

There was a tremendous rupture of some kind, totally unprecedented, or else it was a rerun of something that had happened many times before, maybe somewhere in space, except no, this rupture created space, at least this time around it did, space and everything in it.

Eons later, a girl kissed Moody Fellow.

I like how scrawny you are, she told him, snapping her bubblegum. That's why I kissed you. Can I borrow your math homework?

Okay, said Moody.

Moody was twelve years old and didn't know much about life. He thought the girl would give him back his homework when she was done with it. If you were as pretty, he reasoned, as this girl was, with her blond hair and everything, why would you need to be dishonest? But this thought was interrupted by another: He'd been kissed! Not on the lips, but still, it was a thing that had never happened before, at least not to him, and now that it had, he felt like the king of all creation.

Take as long as you need with the homework, he said, handing it over.

The girl flashed him a smile and took off down the hall. She never kissed Moody again, or spoke to him, or gave him back his homework.

It made him mad that she didn't give it back. But he didn't tell anyone he was mad.

3

A few days after that first kiss, Moody rode his bike out into the countryside to do what he did best, which was to sit and think about stuff and not really figure it out.

Be careful, dear, called his mother from the yard as he wheeled his red nine-speed (the tenth was broken) down the drive and into the street. Moody loved his mother the way he loved the sun: he'd sure miss her if she were gone, which was inconceivable. It seemed fitting to Moody that the sun and his mother collaborated in the preparation of his meals. First the sun made plants grow; then his mother chopped up those plants and sautéed them, or chopped up the already chopped-up parts of animals that had eaten the plants—you get the idea.

Moody loved his father too; he did the dishes.

Arf! said the family dog from the fenced-in area of the yard, where she was running madly in circles. Moody and his brothers had named the dog Bloke even though she was a girl dog. This was classic Fellow family humor.

Moody pedaled away up the street. It was a nice enough street, and Moody loved it, for it was the only street in the world that was his. To us narrators, though, there was nothing special about it, and we're not going to bother describing it. Moody rode up a hill, then down the other side in a rush, and lo! he was no longer in the suburbs. For yea, he was in the countryside. And his heart was glad.

Plenty of trouble lay ahead in Moody's life, and he would find it harder and harder as the years went by to conjure his former enthusiasm for the world as it showed itself just then: the gold-green sunlit meadow alongside which he now coasted on his nine-speed, the whimsical little one-lane stone bridge over the local creek, whose babbling, although it was exactly like the babbling of any other creek in the world, seemed to Moody an original song meant just for him. He crested the little bridge and on the other side dismounted, let his nine-speed fall to the grass by the road, and flopped down in his favorite spot on the bank of the creek and began thinking about elves.

Yes, elves. Moody half believed in them, you see. He half thought that they were everywhere, at least in the countryside, keeping always just out of sight, living quiet, watchful, graceful lives, not hurrying, not paving things, not talking too loud—not doing all the annoying and/or down-right wrong things humans did. Moody even half believed that he himself might be an elf. No doubt he'd gotten the idea from a book. In any case it pleased him to imagine himself secretly in league with secret beings who appreciated the finer things in life, like the way the sunlight this afternoon broke itself into pieces in the dark waters of the creek, never to be reassembled.

Sitting in the warm sunshine by the cool, rushing creek, Moody could concentrate on how pretty the blond-haired girl was and how she'd kissed him totally out of the blue—and never mind about the math homework. Maybe she too was secretly an elf, he thought. Or maybe they could run away together and go looking for elves. The truth is, Moody had only the haziest pictures in his mind as far as love was concerned. They were always awash in sunlight, the pictures, or else maybe they *were* sunlight. One thing Moody was sure of, though, from books: love always brought out the best in people.

Poor Moody. He really wasn't cut out for the world as we know it.

4

Of course, the world as we know it might be only the world as we think we know it, not the world as it actually is—a world that in any case is forever being devoured by the world as it will be, however that may be, and then shat out in the form of the world as it was, however that may have been. Three of these worlds—the world as it will be, the world as it was, and the world as we think we know it—receive a lot more love letters than the world as it actually is. That's just how it is.

Whether this novel is a love letter and, if so, to what world it is addressed are questions that will be answered, if at all, later.

5

Nor are we as yet prepared to answer the question of Amanda or even to say exactly what that question might be. Amanda was a girl about Moody's age but well north of his latitude: she lived on the tundra in a one-room shack with her father, who blamed her—unfairly, he knew—for her mother's death in childbirth. Sometimes Amanda's father was gentle with her, but on other occasions he made her carry firewood late at night in the cold and then carry it back to where she'd gotten it. You're as pretty as your mother was, he would tell her, but it's not enough to be pretty. You also have to be strong.

Strong or not, Amanda was, truth be told, far prettier than her mother had been. We happen to know, in fact, that she was destined to become one of the most beautiful women who'd ever lived. One day, in a sign of things to come, the eleven-year-old Amanda was out walking under a vast sky and humming a tune when a songbird dropped out of the blue and landed with a quiet, grateful thud on the earth by her well-formed feet. Oh no, thought Amanda, but in her heart she knew the bird's death was a tribute to her beauty—and she was glad.

Amanda daydreamed about running away from home and becoming an artist. She made mental lists of the things she would pack in her duffel bag—wool socks, an iron bracelet that flattered not only the wrist it was on but also somehow the other wrist, a jar of maple syrup in case she needed some quick calories—but she kept putting off actually packing the bag, much less leaving, because she couldn't get past the image she had of her father sitting alone in his chair by the woodstove, wondering, as the wind rattled the roof of the shack, what he'd done to drive away his only living relative.

I'll never leave you, Daddy, she would say to him sometimes when he was in one of his gentle moods. But she knew it was a lie.

Moody's second kiss foisted itself upon him four years after the first. It happened on a Wednesday, in the wake of algebra. The bestower of the kiss was an awkward girl Moody'd been informed liked him, as in *liked*. He'd been avoiding her, but now here she was, upon him in the hallway. His main concern as she leaned toward him pursing her anemic lips and squeezing shut her eyes, which when open were slightly crossed, was to make sure no one who mattered witnessed the event. Those who mattered numbered three: Moody's best friend, Tall Jim; his second-best friend, Jorge, an exchange student who was Moody's doubles partner on the tennis team; and, three, the girl on whom Moody at that time had a crush, a skinny girl with explosive hair, an extensive collection of brightly colored miniskirts, and a name that doesn't matter anymore, though it did at the time, quite a bit, to Moody and, presumably, to the girl herself, else she wouldn't have changed it after graduation. She had the locker next to Moody's, and one of the reasons Moody liked her so much (in addition to how he was struck speechless, though not literally struck, by her amazing limbs, all four, and not literally speechless either) was that although she could outpeck him in terms of the social pecking order, she always, when the two of them happened to be at their lockers at the same time, had a friendly word for him. And not always a mere word—

sometimes they had actual conversations, the sort in which views were exchanged. Moody learned, for instance, that this girl believed the space-time continuum was like a many-colored soap bubble, its colors constantly shifting, which seemed about right to him, god how he wanted to kiss her. When they crossed paths elsewhere than at their lockers, she ignored him. It was as though she too were struck speechless, but not in a good way.

While he scanned the hallway for the three who mattered, Moody managed to angle his face away from the approaching face of the awkward girl, so that her lips would meet not his lips but, say, his cheek or, as it turned out, his jawbone, or rather the skin that kept it mercifully from view. She didn't seem nearly as awkward from close up, he noticed as he turned away. There was a mole-like blindness as she came at him with eyes closed that stirred within him something tenderer and less sure of itself than pity would have been. Whatever it was, it wasn't desire, as the girl saw clearly when she opened her eyes to the post-kiss universe. The ache she felt was no less painful for being something nearly everyone who has ever lived has experienced.

I have to go to history, Moody said.

I'm sorry, said the girl.

You're okay, said Moody, not knowing what he meant by it but knowing he intended it as a kindness. Then he hurried away, relieved that those who mattered hadn't seen.

7

Around this time, Moody explained to his piano teacher that although it might be true that other people needed to practice the piano in order to get good at it, he, Moody Fellow, did not intend to approach music in quite that way.

I've noticed that, said his piano teacher, a short, solid woman who was six decades Moody's senior and had heard this kind of thing before.

I want to play by pure feeling, Moody said. I want to play by inspiration, you know, in the moment.

Moody meant what he was saying. He thought people like Beethoven had been struck by the lightning bolt of pure musical feeling and had created beautiful music on the spot, while still warm from the lightning bolt. And he wanted to be the same way when he played Beethoven. Surely the great man deserved no less.

I'm not here to teach you musical feeling, said Moody's piano teacher. You have that already. I'm here to teach you how to work.

Moody didn't want to work, at least not at music. He worked at tennis. It didn't occur to him to try to play a tennis match based on pure, in-the-moment feeling, with no preparation. No, what had made him the second-best player on his high school team, behind his doubles partner Jorge, were the thousands of hours he'd spent on tennis courts, endlessly running, hitting ball after ball to different spots on the court, with different spins, at different speeds, with different goals in mind. None of this seemed like work to Moody, for he loved every moment of it. He loved the sounds of the game—the pock! of the ball being struck, the squeak! of a player's sneaker as he or she abruptly changed direction. He loved the sport's Euclidean geometry and the way it was a contest of wills. He was, he would later think, both physically and psychologically addicted to tennis. He didn't see why anyone else wouldn't love it too, for instance girls. In a sign of how poorly he understood those fair and mysterious creatures, he thought he was more likely to win girls' admiration by scooting back and forth along the baseline, getting every ball back deep with topspin, than he was by performing the first movement of the Moonlight Sonata, which, because he rarely practiced, he couldn't play very well.

In tennis, love equals zero. But although our teenage protagonist lost his share of tennis matches, that is not what we mean when we say that, before he died, a moody fellow named Moody Fellow found love.

8

Nor are we referring to the first time a girl Moody liked liked him back. This finally happened about a year after the awkward girl had kissed him. Moody, seventeen now, was on a field trip to the countryside. His biology class had gone to a pig farm to see what things were done there and how. Moody didn't give a rip about pigs. He spent the day thinking about hitting passing shots down the line (a higher art, to his way of thinking, than hitting them crosscourt) and glancing not so furtively at Jane McConnell's cute, freckled face and the lively brown hair that framed it and also at her collarbone and so on. Moody liked Jane because there was something immediately present about her; she had an air about her, an intelligence or something. Anyway, he thought she was cute, even if, as Tall Jim and Jorge didn't hesitate to point out to him, she had a pear-shaped figure. What have you got against pears? Moody would say in response, or else simply: No, she doesn't. But she did, he could see. But so what?

Today, pig day, it seemed to Moody that Jane McConnell was returning his not-so-furtive glances. This made him happier than anyone else who'd ever lived had ever been. It was as though each of Jane McConnell's glances his way were a sun that shone only on him, or only for him, or only, it may not be too much to say, in him. Indeed, let us say more, for this was one of the great moments of

Moody's life. Each of Jane's glances at Moody that day was an exploding star, and he, Moody Fellow, was, in each case, that same star, blasting itself to happy smithereens with the help of Jane McConnell's cute brown eyes.

One reason Moody was so happy was that there was some stuff of which he was not yet aware. He didn't yet know, for instance, that Jane McConnell's parents, the McConnells, had died in a plane crash when she was five. He didn't know that Jane and her seven sisters were all, individually and as a group, kind of messed up, partly as a result of that plane crash, partly because of their genes, partly because of the degraded state of the culture at large during the time period in question, and partly for no known reason. Nor, and more to the point, did Moody know that in a few short weeks, after he and Jane will have started dating but before they'll have come anywhere near doing what is sometimes known as the deed, Jane will in fact do that deed, not with Moody but with a football player nicknamed Grizzly, on the floor of the bathroom at a house where there'll be a party Moody won't be able to attend because he'll be out of town with his family visiting relatives who won't think Moody or his brothers quite old enough yet to drink root beer. Moody will arrive at school on Monday not having heard what Jane did on Saturday night, though many others will have heard. It'll fall to Tall Jim to tell Moody, over chicken fingers after school. Moody will know something's up when Tall Jim pays for Moody's chicken fingers. They will be the first things Tall Jim has ever bought for anyone whose name is not Tall Jim. Something I got to tell you, man, Tall Jim will say between bites of his own chicken fingers. Something about Jane.

But of course Moody will feel as though what Jane has done is not about her at all but is instead about him, a judgment on him. As though she were letting him know what kind of man he wasn't.

Life, in short, was about to throw Moody for a serious loop.

Which ain't to say, though, that he shouldn't have been exactly as elated as he was when, on the bus ride back from the pig farm, Jane McConnell sat her ample seat down next to his scrawny one and said, Hey.

9

One day Amanda came home from a wild walk in the wind and found her father slumped dead in his chair by the woodstove. Oh, Daddy, she said as she closed his eyes.

She packed her duffel bag and walked the mile and a half to the home of the nearest neighbor, a Mrs. Quinn. She told Mrs. Quinn that her father was dead and she was running away to become an artist. You're too young for that, dear, Mrs. Quinn told her, and Amanda, realizing it was true, began crying. Mrs. Quinn made her some hot chocolate and then went into another room and placed two phone calls: one to the tundra's coroner and another to its orphanage.

Everything will be just fine, honey, said Mrs. Quinn as she went back into the room where Amanda sat sniffling over her cocoa. Such a beautiful girl, Mrs. Quinn thought. Beautiful but unlucky.

Would you like another cup? she said to the girl.

Amanda started to shake her head no, but then it occurred to her that from now on she could have—and do and be—whatever she wanted.

Yes, please, she said.

10

The day after Tall Jim bought him an order of chicken fingers, Moody played the best singles match of his high school tennis career. His opponent was a lefty he didn't care for because the guy pumped his fist theatrically every time he won a point. Moody had played him once before and beaten him, but it had been a close match, hard fought, a bit rough around the edges. This time was different. Moody kept the ball to his opponent's weaker backhand side and enjoyed watching him self-destruct. Moody felt light and strong and quick, and it seemed that wherever he wanted the ball to go, it went. The whole thing was immensely satisfying, or would have been if he hadn't been too distracted to enjoy it.

Why did she do it? he asked himself as he approached the net and angled a volley winner. What can she have been thinking? he thought, punching a return at the feet of his hapless opponent. It was three days since Jane's indiscretion, and Moody hadn't yet spoken with her. She'd missed the past two days of school and hadn't returned the phone call Moody had placed the day before. Moody wasn't angry, or if he was, he didn't know it yet. Instead he thought of the incident as a problem he had to solve. He was good at solving problems; he'd won his class's math award in ninth grade, if only because Frank Salvatore hadn't turned in all his homework. Surely the question of why the first girl who ever liked Moody back had immediately betrayed him was one to which he, Moody Fellow, could work out the answer. There couldn't be that many variables.

By the time he ambled to the net to shake hands with his humiliated opponent, Moody had arrived at a hypothesis: Jane had done the deed with Grizzly (and what was it like, Moody wondered, to do the deed?) because she didn't understand how much he, Moody, cared about her. Which was a lot, as far as Moody could tell. After all, Jane was the first girl who'd ever French-kissed him. She's just depressed! Moody told himself. She doesn't get that I would do anything for her—even something dangerous, maybe, if she asked me to.

That night he again called her on the phone.

Oh, Moody, Jane said when she answered.

I care about you a lot, Moody said. Don't you see? It doesn't matter what happened. I think you're just depressed—

Moody, said Jane, you're a nice guy, but you don't have a clue about anything.

Moody pictured Jane sitting on the porch swing on the patio at the back of the house in which her aunt and uncle had raised her and her sisters badly. A week ago, he'd been there with her on that swing. They'd French-kissed. He'd found it exciting. Maybe she hadn't.

I have a clue about some things, Moody said.

Jane sighed. Goodbye, Moody. I'm sorry it happened this way, but it had to happen. Nice guys get hurt. You should try being less nice.

Do you want to go to the carnival next week? Moody said, but the line was dead.

II

Amanda, who'd been raised far from other children and for that matter had little idea how to behave around adults who weren't her father, was at first piercingly uncomfortable in her new life at the orphanage. For the first time she became aware of the effect her beauty had on other people. To walk into a room was, she observed, to bring to an immediate halt whatever had been going on there. People stared at her in a way that was several orders of magnitude more intense than the way they stared at other pretty girls. In the beginning, Amanda couldn't shake the feeling that it was her fault all those eyes were pinned to her. I've done something wrong, haven't I? she would think.

One day it occurred to her that if she was going to go through life feeling as if she'd done something wrong, she might as well do something wrong. So she took a pan of cornbread from the orphanage's kitchen and put it on the ground by the front door of the main building and then stomped on it with her feet, which were in boots. She didn't care who saw her, and in fact the headmaster, an old man who'd seen just about every variety of adolescent misbehavior but never before anything involving cornbread, was the first on the scene.

What are you doing, you beautiful girl? he said.

Oh, just stomping on the cornbread, said Amanda.

Hmm, said the headmaster. Everything okay?

I think it's a little boring here, said Amanda.

No doubt you're right, said the headmaster, smiling a little, in spite of himself, at how wondrously well the girl's ethereal childish beauty was beginning to ripen into the earthier beauty of a surpassingly desirable young woman. Good god, he thought, I haven't had a sexual thought in a decade. He went away humming a tune about forgiving the young their trespasses.

From then on, Amanda did whatever she felt like doing. She skipped two-thirds of her lessons, refused to make her bed, and lost her virginity one day in a haystack to a boy who'd lost his the year before in the same haystack to a girl who couldn't remember ever having been a virgin, because she couldn't remember anything, because ever since her parents had died in a wheat-farming accident she hadn't wanted to remember anything, and what she didn't want to do she didn't do. (Turning out girls who did only what they wanted to, or didn't what they didn't, was one of the orphanage's specialties.)

I love you! shouted the boy in the haystack at the exact moment he was finishing what Amanda had started.

No, no, no, Amanda said. That is not what this is.

The boy extracted himself, wiped a tear from his eye, and said, Well, what is it then?

I don't know, said Amanda as she stood and refastened her overalls. But I aim to find out.

In the next few months, Amanda liaised, if that is a word, with every boy at the orphanage and several of the men, plus a girl or two. Concluding that sex was uninteresting, at least on the tundra, she got down to work trying to become an artist. She figured this involved: a) brooding; b) holding in contempt all institutions, persons, and ideas outside the self; and c) trying to learn how to draw people's facial features. She had a knack for the first two activities but not the third, and she was just about to turn her back once and for all on her artistic ambitions when one day, without warning, she made, almost by accident, a brilliantly expressive sculpture. The orphan girls' math tutor, a gaunt and ghostly fellow with a hunted or haunted look about the eyes, had told her she was a blockhead. No one had ever spoken to Amanda that way before. She knew she wasn't a blockhead—she merely hadn't felt like giving the right answer to the question the tutor had asked—and so the insult didn't sting. Instead it produced a curious effect: it caused her to look more closely at the tutor. He had an unusually narrow chin, deep-set, hollow-looking eyes, and a prominent, unevenly contoured forehead. His mouth seemed wetter than it should have and was thoroughly unpleasant to behold; it was more an open wound than a mouth. Even so, the overall effect of the tutor's face might have been somehow redeemed by a strong, angular nose, but alas, the man's nose was a girlish little button that seemed to be trying to hide amid the wreckage around it.

Here is a face no human heart could love,

thought Amanda. Here is a man careening through the world utterly alone. He lives alone. He'll die alone. He'll be forgotten. The only one who can't forget him is him, which is ironic because his greatest wish is to forget himself for just a few minutes.

So moved was Amanda by this first-ever glimpse into the agony of a soul not her own that she stood up in a daze and wandered out of the building and off onto the tundra. (The math tutor felt bad—he assumed she'd left because he'd called her a blockhead—but what could you do, his nerves were frayed, if only he could get a little time away from the wife and kid, not that he didn't love them, of course, and in fact the thought of his little boy made him smile: the lad was the spitting image of his old man.) The world is a world of pain and longing, Amanda thought, and as she walked she gathered tundra grasses and twiggy scrub plants. It was a cold day, gray and windy, the usual. Amanda took the grasses and twiggy scrub plants back to her room and, still in a compassion-induced daze, assembled them into an incredibly lifelike representation of the math tutor. The way the grass-and-twig figure slumped made you want to care for it even as you wished you'd never laid eyes on it, ugly thing that it was. It still needed a head. For this, Amanda used a small wooden block that she took from the young orphans' playpen. When she set the block atop the grass-and-twig figure, the effect was stunning. All night Amanda sat staring at her first successful work of art.

This is what I am meant to do, she thought.

Her next half dozen sculptures were failures, however, and in despair she started smoking cigarettes. One day as she was puffing on one in a stylish way under the eaves of the main building, or one of the eaves—what is an eave, anyway?—the headmaster rounded a corner and, seeing the world's most beautiful fifteen-year-old girl striking a sophisticated pose that ought to have been a few years beyond her, clutched his chest and fell to the ground a dead man.

Amanda coolly regarded the old man's inert form, took a drag on her cigarette, and then said quietly, I accept your tribute.

Only when she had finished her cigarette did she call for help.

12

A few years later, in the City—for yes, this is on its way to becoming an urban novel—a group of neocubist artists calling themselves the New Cubists started building a bunch of new cubes. Some of the cubes were made of wood, some of plastic, some of glass or stone. They were of every different size and were painted many different colors, or were not painted, or were painted but not with colored paint. They were all the same shape. Once made, they were placed in strategic locations throughout the City, or perhaps there was no strategy; perhaps (who could say?) there was no City.

Whether the cubes had a purpose was for a long time unknown beyond the ranks of the New Cubists. Some noncubists said the cubes seemed to want to say something about what kind of city the City had become. Others said that although the cubes had many things to tell the City, the City would never get to hear these things, either because the cubes didn't know how to speak or because the City didn't know how to listen. A third contingent held that no cube anywhere had ever had anything to say except: Cube. Which was plenty to ponder, in this contingent's opinion.

We narrators have always felt there was something a little creepy about the cubes. Say you're alone on an underground train platform late at night; you look to your left, and there sits, or stands, a small red wooden cube, seemingly waiting for the train you're waiting for. The seconds pass like centuries, an entire age defined by the awkward silence that pulses in the air between you and the cube.

Or suppose you enter the local branch of your regional or national bank and find yourself in line behind a large cube of thick, clear glass. You know what to do—politely step around the cube and proceed to the teller's window—but the experience is disconcerting, even frightening, though obscurely so.

Art can be dangerous, as both Moody Fellow and Amanda would one day discover.

Moody arrived at a small liberal arts college on the outskirts of the City feeling like the only college freshman in the history of the world who hadn't yet done the deed. Jane McConnell had taken from him his innocence but not his virginity—rotten luck. The good news was that, over the summer, he'd been granted the unsolicited oral, as opposed to verbal, attentions of a disheveled-looking girl to whose house he'd delivered a pizza. That was his summer job, delivering pizzas; he wasn't just carrying pizzas around town and knocking on doors as a leisure activity, though if he'd thought he could meet a girl that way and perhaps find love with her, he might've tried it. It was amazing, of course, his first blowjob, and he fell in love with the girl on the spot, even though her hair was a bit stringy and the lenses of her glasses were badly scratched and she was missing an arm. But when he told her of his feelings, she said would he please zip up now and was it okay that she didn't have any money for a tip? Of course it's okay, my gosh, said Moody. He was astounded to learn that girls like this, or at least one girl like this, existed. He went to the door but stopped at the doorway and turned and grinned goofily at the girl, trying not to stare at where her arm wasn't.

Go, said the girl.

He went—all the way to college, as was noted. He planned to study philosophy and one day become a philosophy professor, the sort who played tennis and maybe the piano in his free time and who had a nice bungalow with a porch on which to sit and watch the rain and think dark but important thoughts and maybe smoke a pipe, the way an uncle of Moody's who was a professor used to before he got emphysema. Moody pictured a vague but beautiful wife living with him in the bungalow, baking a lot of bread and maybe doing something artistic. She would be a little bit elflike. They would have energetic sex, whatever that meant, and she would never, ever cheat on him, or he on her.

Yet no sooner did Moody begin the academic study of philosophy than he became disillusioned with the academic study of philosophy. He couldn't believe all these philosophers had really believed the things they claimed to believe. David Hume, for instance, insisted it couldn't be proved that the sun was any more likely to rise on the morrow than not to rise, and Moody thought: Really? This seemed to Moody like the thought process of a man who was trying to avoid doing or thinking about something more pressing.

And there were indeed things in the world that pressed more. The cantankerous country of which Moody was a citizen was threatening to bomb a distant land for the sake of peace. This made Moody angry, but what made him angrier was that it didn't seem to make most other people angry. Wake up! he wanted to say to his countrymen. He told his parents over the phone that the nation was sleepwalking toward an act so immoral—

Keep your head down, said Moody's father, and focus on your studies.

But we're talking about mass death here, Moody said.

It's very upsetting, said Moody's mother after a pause. But, honey, try to keep things in perspective. Write your representative a letter, but don't let yourself get too worked up about it.

Your job right now is to do well in school, said Moody's father.

Some things are more important than other things, Moody said.

That's what we're trying to tell you, said his father. But I have to go to the bathroom now. Goodbye.

His father hung up the receiver.

You know he's just worried about you, said Moody's mother.

Moody joined the campus antiwar group. Right away he fell in love with most of the girls who were involved. Their eyes were so bright, was the main thing, but it didn't hurt that a number of them had excellent figures. They insisted on being called women. Call me whatever you like, Moody wanted to say, but instead he said things like, Let's throw a wrench into the gears of the war machine.

How? said a girl called Daphne. She was the one Moody liked best. Her laugh was as clear as a bell, though it didn't in other respects sound like a bell, and she wore a bandanna in her hair most days in a way that drove Moody quietly crazy. Now she looked at him eagerly.

Um, Moody said. I think—

We have to take this fight directly to the Man, said a fellow named Pablo. Pablo didn't shower very often, Moody'd noticed. Daphne didn't seem to mind, he'd also noticed.

The question, said a gaunt-faced fellow with spiked hair and a dog collar around his neck, is, Do we fight fire with fire? Or do we deceive ourselves into believing that it can be fought with water?

Define your terms, someone else said.

The war went ahead in spite of the long hours the antiwar group at Moody's college spent defining its terms. It was a quick war, fought mostly from the air, but even so a lot of people died, many of them horrifically, and for what? Moody's group did score one coup when it illegally hung a giant PEACE banner from a highway overpass. A number of drivers honked their horns and gave the thumbs-up, which made Moody feel that perhaps there was hope for his country after all—just not very much.

One day, after the war was over, Moody decided he would pay Daphne a visit in her dorm room. He wanted to talk to her about his feelings about the war and about how history didn't seem to proceed in any one direction. His hands shook as he walked across the campus under a blue sky. He reached her dorm, went up to the third floor, and knocked on her door. Pablo answered. His bare torso was soaked in sweat. He offered Moody a beer.

Where's Daphne? Moody said, but as he said it he saw her in a corner of the room, bending to pull a slipper onto one of her feet. She wore only a silken robe, and as she bent, Moody got a good look at her breasts, about which Pablo obviously knew a lot more than Moody ever would.

Moody! said Daphne in a friendly voice while with a hand she pulled her robe shut.

Moody left and went to play the piano in a practice room in the music building. He hadn't played in quite a while, but now the music gushed from him in a torrent. He played pieces by Chopin, who died young, Brahms, who loved his mentor's wife, and Scriabin, a madman. Moody played by pure feeling—he was totally in the moment. He played poorly, but it felt good to play.

There's been a war, he thought (picturing the charred corpses that day's newspaper had shown), but we're all supposed to just get on with our lives as if nothing had happened.

It was his first real lesson in philosophy.

14

The man who would soon become, though he didn't know this yet, the founder of the New Cubists was an artist who no longer went by his given name, Jason Applethorn. The job of an artist, after all, was to take what was given and make of it something truer or at least more beautiful. Applethorn's truer or more beautiful name was Chad.

Chad was a middle-aged man with the beginnings of a belly and something beyond the beginnings of lower-back trouble. He sat, when sculpting, upon an ergonomically excellent stool/chair fashioned for him a few years earlier by a friend/lover who'd since died in a bizarre train accident. (Or perhaps you don't find anything bizarre about a train's having plunged from a high trestle to the floor of the valley three hundred feet below, where a certain unlucky furniture designer, rest his soul, was out for an afternoon stroll.) Chad worried from time to time that having so comfortable a seat on which to sit when sculpting might drain his work of the urgency and edginess that, to be frank, it had never had enough of to begin with. Perhaps this fear helps explain why his mind's eye was drawn to the edgy edges and urgent right angles of what was for him a new form.

You see, Chad hadn't always been a cubist, much less a neocubist. If you'd told him that he would soon be regarded as the founder of an artistic movement called New Cubism, he would have stared at you and said nothing, but what he would've been thinking was, Why are you making fun of me? Chad's earlier forays into artmaking, which had involved spheres and icosahedrons as well as the occasional line drawing, had been almost universally ignored, even by him. At one point he'd given up art entirely and taken a job as a file clerk at a low-cost health clinic. But the urge to create was much stronger in him than the urge to alphabetize, and soon he was spending nights after work in his rented studio pursuing the image that had for some time been beckoning to him from the corner of his mind's eye.

That image was of a granite cube painted sky blue. Why sky blue? Why granite? Why a cube? Chad wasn't the sort of artist who interrogated his mind's eye. He did what the eye told him to do, and that was that.

So he ordered a block of granite from a stone merchant and, once it was delivered, set about hewing the stone into the shape of a cube. This he was able to do while taking his ease upon his ergonomic seat, for he happened to own a stone-cutting machine. It was very loud, and when he used it he wore earplugs that made him feel even more lost inside his head, and more alone in the world, than he usually did, which was saying something. In Chad's case it came close to saying everything.

Except no, to have said everything about Chad one would also have had to mention the strange fierceness that animated this bleary-eyed, slightly doughy man. Also worthy of note was the chronic sadness that had been his nearest companion in life ever since his mother had abandoned him, not on purpose, in favor of oblivion. The sadness came in waves that washed not over him but right through him, through the center of him. He secretly believed that his greatest gift to the world would be to take that sadness with him when he was buried.

When he finished cutting the stone, Chad painted all fifty-four square feet of its surface sky blue. He drew back and solemnly regarded his work. Then, in spite of himself, or perhaps even to spite himself, he smiled.

In the months after the war, Moody became a moodier fellow than he'd ever been before. When he was happy—say, when he was hanging out with his friends late at night, discussing urgent political or metaphysical questions while tearing through box after box of speedily delivered pizza—he was so happy that he thought he might float out the window and off into the freedom of the night sky, like a happy balloon. More often, however, he was a balloon that couldn't make itself get out of bed in the morning and brush its teeth and haul itself up the hill to economics class. If only he could lose his virginity, Moody figured, he would spend more time feeling buoyant. Or maybe the problem was rooted in international geopolitics, in which case Moody might remain a sad balloon for years to come.

He didn't feel able to talk with his parents about his moods, for there was something shameful, he felt, in having become a moodier fellow than the one they'd delivered to the campus mere months earlier. For the first time in his life, Moody wondered why his parents had named him Moody. (In fact they'd told him why years earlier—he had an ancestor named Moody, an unsmiling frontier dentist—but he'd been too young to absorb the information.) His brothers were Jack and Eli, after all—far less adjectival names than the one Moody'd been saddled with.

But here I am these days, earning my name,

Moody thought, and the thought was like a dark curtain that descended between him and his former sense of himself as not all that moody a fellow.

Only when he played the piano did Moody feel at ease with his newfound moodiness. He played four times a week. All his life he'd been playing from sheet music; now he began improvising. If he was in a dark mood, he played something dark. If he felt happy or playful, he let that fact be known, if only to himself, via the notes he played and the order he played them in. There may have been nothing groundbreaking about Moody's improvisations, but they did undeniably allow him to express himself to himself, which is a harder thing to come by in life than is generally supposed, though it may also be less valuable than people tend to think.

The point is, Moody was becoming himself, or the most up-to-date version thereof. Which was all to the good. Yet he was as lonely as an involuntary hermit on the north face of the world's most godforsaken mountain. Come down off that mountain, Moody! Come to the lowlands and join, if you can find it, the party.

16

Breasts! She had them, and they were nice, and Moody was looking at them now in the moonlight, because, incredibly, here he was, skinnydipping at midnight in a pool behind a small-town monastery with a girl from college whose smile was utterly dazzling—a woman, rather—and who had a real sense of fun and aliveness (was how Moody put it to himself) and who hadn't yet kissed him but surely mightn't be averse to the idea, although who could say? Her nipples were larger than others he'd seen. It had been her idea to go skinny-dipping. The monks are all asleep, she'd said. The small town they were in was the one she'd grown up in with the help of her very single, very spiritual mother, and Moody, a friend from college or, he hoped, more than a friend, had been invited for a visit. This girl/woman had a lot of energy, nearly all of it positive, as far as Moody knew, and she also had a name, which was Clara. Being in her presence made Moody feel that for the first time in his life he was blood-pumpingly, skin-tinglingly alive—something that in truth had happened before on a number of occasions.

They'd met in an anthropology class about social upheaval. Social upheaval was spoken of in this class as though it were invariably a good thing, a kind of electroshock therapy that societies administered to themselves about one-third as often as it was needed. The professor teaching the course was an expatriate from a nation that had won its independence just a few months earlier. Political opponents were being disappeared by the new nation's government; the professor could barely contain his excitement.

The masks, he said to his uneasy students, fall away, do they not?

Moody noticed Clara on the first day of class. She wore white jeans and brown hiking boots and a gray sweatshirt emblazoned with the name of a rival college. Her hair was glorious, falling as it did in thick dark curls around her lovely, olive-skinned face. Moody felt guilty about noticing that she had a nice body, for women weren't objects, he'd learned. One wasn't even supposed to daydream about them as objects, because such retrograde thoughts would leak out from one's mind—Moody wasn't certain of the mechanism by which this happened—and poison the world politically, which was the last thing the world needed.

During that first class period, Clara raised her hand and said something about exuberance and the life force as they related to social upheaval. What she was saying made sense at first, Moody thought, but then a moment later it didn't anymore, and, good heavens, what did she mean when she said that matter wasn't really real? Which, even if it were in some sense true—for how could one say for sure what was real and what wasn't?—what did it have to do with social upheaval?

After class, Moody fell into step beside Clara, who moved with a dancer's or athlete's grace, and asked her what she'd meant about the unreality of matter. In response she smiled a smile that melted something hard and cold in Moody—something like ice, we see from how we've described it, though of course it wasn't really ice.

Join me for coffee? she said.

They obtained two cups of the stuff in the usual manner at the village coffee shop. Moody drank his black. Clara doctored hers with milk and an astonishing amount of sugar. They sat at a table in the corner.

Where are you from? Moody said.

Clara told him the name of the town she'd grown up in. Moody said he'd never heard of it. Then she asked where he was from, and he told her, and she said she'd never heard of it, and then they both sort of looked at their coffee and blew on it, and Moody thought he could hear Clara tapping one of her hiking boots against the hardwood floor.

So you're interested in philosophy, Moody said.

I am? said Clara.

Matter isn't really real? he said.

Oh, Clara said, and she waved a hand dismissively. That's not philosophy. That's just part of my religion.

What's your religion? said Moody. I mean, if you want to talk about it?

He sort of hoped she didn't want to. Religion made him nervous.

My religion is based on a true understanding of what is and is not real, said Clara. But tell me about yourself.

Moody told Clara that he loved the country-side next to which he'd grown up; that as a boy he'd believed in elves, or half believed in them; that his family's dog Bloke, a girl, was old and could barely walk and was in pain and soon might have to be helped to die, which his mother was very upset about; and that he thought the war had been fought for some dark purpose and not for the brighter one the government had invoked publicly.

What kind of elves? Clara said.

Quiet ones, Moody said.

That's cute, Clara said.

Moody wanted to say, You're cute. But he figured Clara probably already knew she was cute, and anyway he didn't want to make her uncomfortable. Nor did he want to make himself any more uncomfortable than he already was. And yet he did just that when, a moment later, he leaned in conspiratorially and said, Which do you think is worse, social upheaval or antisocial tranquility?

He had thought the remark clever, maybe even profound, before he'd uttered it aloud, but now he was certain it was neither, and he could see by the almost stricken look on Clara's face that she agreed with his second opinion.

Oh! she said after a moment, setting her coffee down. I forgot I had a dentist's appointment at three. See you next time in class!

She got up and smiled a smile that didn't look as if it needed any repair work. Then she turned gracefully on her heel and strode away.

Moody watched her go. Idiot, he thought, meaning himself.

17

But even an idiot can try to get what he wants in life. Sometimes he can even succeed.

Moody kept after Clara, and before long they were hanging out pretty regularly, talking about social upheaval and Clara's religion and Moody's feelings about war and history and mental clutter. From there it was a short figurative distance to the literal pool behind the very real monastery in the town in which Clara had grown up. Let's rejoin them there. Remember, they're naked.

It's a beautiful night, Moody said, wishing he were taller so he wouldn't have to hop awkwardly on tiptoe to keep his nose and mouth above the water.

Clara's smile gleamed in the moonlight as she paddled toward him.

Oh! Moody said when Clara took hold of a part of his material body that was already alert. He hoped she thought it was real.

Moody, she said, pressing herself against him. Let's have sex.

In the pool? he said.

Sure, she said.

Shouldn't we kiss first? said Moody. I mean, we've never even kissed.

Well, kiss me then, said Clara.

Moody kissed her. Her lips were very nice.

Now we do the other thing, Clara said.

It's a little deep here, said Moody.

She took him by the hand and led him to shallower water.

It's your first time, isn't it? she said.

Moody just looked at her, the water streaming off her thick hair and down her beautiful shoulders. He was trembling.

It's my first time too, she said with an inscrutable smile.

Moody eyed the monastery, which loomed black against the moonlit sky.

You're sure the monks aren't—?

All they do is sleep, she said. Here, let's climb out and do it on the grass.

Terribly excited and also simply terrified, Moody clambered out of the pool after Clara and sort of tackled her on the grass and began awkwardly humping her in a very unfocused way. He hoped she would take the lead.

Put it in, she said, guiding him with her hand and closing her eyes.

Moody tried to put it in, but it wouldn't go in.

Does it hurt? he said.

Go slowly, Clara said.

He went slowly.

Don't stop completely, she said. Just go—like this.

A cricket chirped nearby. There were no lights on in any of the monastery windows. Clara moved slowly under him, her eyes closed and an expression on her face that said to leave her alone, she was concentrating. For his part, Moody felt as though he were trying to poke a hole in a wall with the most sensitive part of his body, which seemed like a bad idea. He was just beginning to worry that he was somehow doing everything wrong, that Clara might laugh at him and tell him to get lost—that maybe Jane McConnell had been right about him all along—when the wall gave way and... oh my... oh no... oh CHRIST!!!

They held still. The cricket seemed very loud to Moody, almost suspiciously loud. Had it been so loud the whole time? Why couldn't it go someplace else?

Clara appeared to be crying.

Was it good for you? Moody said, and he reached out to touch her hair.

Pull out, she said, turning her face from his touch.

Moody pulled out, then hugged Clara as best he could while she turned away from him and pressed her face into the grass.

At length Moody said, We should have used a—

Shh, said Clara.

She wiped the tears from her face, sat up, and smiled a wan smile Moody found beautiful and very touching, even though—or perhaps because—he had no idea what thoughts were going through her head. Why had she cried? He didn't know. Why had she given herself to him? He didn't know that either. He would never know these things.

Clara stood and went over to retrieve her clothes. Moody felt as though he were a movie actor watching the woman with whom he'd just had movie sex pull on her panties, then her shorts, then her bra and, finally, her T-shirt. It occurred to him that the difference was that a movie actor in that situation wouldn't actually have had sex (depending on what type of movie), whereas he, Moody Fellow, had, for the first and, he hoped, not the last time, done just that—i.e., the deed. He guessed, correctly, that he hadn't done it as well or for as long as might have been appreciated, but still, it was a step in the right direction, a sizable step, and he intended to keep walking in that direction. He hoped Clara would accompany him.

The big white moon shone down on the lawn like a stage light. The air was sweet—we forgot to mention this before—with the scent of honeysuckle.

Let's do that again sometime, Moody said when Clara came over to him with his clothes bunched in her hands.

Listen to you, she said, handing him her clothes. Now get dressed and let's see if the ice cream stand is still open.

18

One night a few weeks later, Moody was clipping his toenails in his dorm room when his mother called and told him that she and his father had taken the sad but necessary decision to put Bloke down.

She'd come to the end of her road, said his mother.

Moody looked at his yellowed toenail clippings in the wastebasket. A minute ago they'd been part of him. Now they were trash.

She had a good life, Moody said.

She sure did, said his mother.

Are you okay? said Moody.

I'm okay, she said. You?

Yeah, said Moody.

He cried later that night, alone in his dorm room, when a memory came to him of Bloke as a vital young dog. It was a sunny day in the memory. Moody and his father and brothers were playing football in the park down by Snyder Creek. Moody's younger brother, Eli, had broken free with the ball and was running toward the end zone when Bloke, seized by inspiration, took off after him. She was like a shaggy missile shooting across the field at her unsuspecting target. Although why bring military imagery into a vignette about a nice time a family spent together? Anyway, at about the ten-yard line Bloke collided with Moody's brother and tripped him up, and down he went.

That's what I call defense! Moody's father had roared.

Before driving Bloke to the vet to be extinguished, Moody's mother had taken her to that same park and sat with her for a while by the creek. Moody pictured the scene, thought of his mother knowing, as Bloke didn't, what came next. It had been weeks since Bloke had been able to walk; Moody's mother must have carried her to where they sat on the grass. Bloke's face had acquired a bewildered look in the last months of her life. Moody wondered whether she'd been totally out of it as she sat on the grass at the park or whether she perked up one last time at the sounds and odors of the outdoors.

Moody wiped his eyes. He didn't know if he was crying for himself, for his mother, or for Bloke. A little of each, he figured.

He reached for the phone and dialed Clara's dorm room.

Hello, she said.

May I come over? said Moody.

I'm busy with my books, said Clara.

My dog died, Moody said.

I'm so sorry, Clara said.

A gust of wind grabbed the treetops outside Moody's dorm-room window and shook them around a bit.

So can I come over? said Moody.

I'm really busy, Moody, said Clara. But we can have lunch tomorrow if you want.

Moody hung up. Let her call back to prove

that she cares, he thought.

For half an hour he sat by the phone, watching the storm-tossed (for yes, there was a thunderstorm) tops of the trees and the lightning-brightened sky and the wet rain. He began to feel sheepish about having hung up. It wasn't the sort of thing he'd been raised to do, and anyway, Clara wasn't even officially his girlfriend, although it was true that since the midnight of skinny-dipping they'd had sex three more times and had even on one occasion gone together to the movies. She was busy with her books. That meant she was holed up with the sacred texts that pertained to her faith, which in Moody's opinion was fraudulent. Even if it wasn't fraudulent, Moody still didn't like it. He doubted whether she could ever be as committed to him as she was to her religion.

Moody put on his shoes and put a breath mint in his mouth and left his dorm room and walked down the hall and down the stairs and out of the building and through the rain to Clara's dorm. He shouldered through the building's front door, or more likely he just pulled it open, and then he walked up the stairs to the fourth floor and made his way down the carpeted hallway to Clara's room. He knocked.

Pablo answered the door. Remember Pablo?

Hey, Moody, said Pablo, grinning. You want a beer?

Moody brushed past him into the room. Clara wasn't busy with her books at all—not unless they were there with her under the covers of her bed.

Moody sat down on the floor. He felt as though three hives' worth of bees were stinging him in the place where his heart would be if he had one, which, even if no one else cared to know it, he did.

First my dog dies, he said. Now this.

Can we talk later? said Clara.

How do you two even know each other? said Moody.

It's a small college, Moody, said Pablo. Would a beer help?

Moody looked at Pablo's narrow, self-satisfied face, his unapologetically unwashed hair, the cowboyish shirt whose top three buttons were undone, revealing a portion of the sweat-shiny skin in which Pablo was, clearly, much more comfortable than Moody would ever be in his.

Fuck you, Pablo, said Moody.

There was a tremendous clap of thunder, but it failed to rattle the dorm's walls, which were made of cinderblock.

Moody, said Clara. I think you should go.

Yeah, said Moody. I think so too.

He stood and took a last look at Clara's luridly beautiful hair spilling this way and that across the open expanse of her pillow—a pillow that had given comfort to Moody's tired head just a few nights ago.

What is it about me? said Moody. Why does this keep happening?

Clara just lay there, not meeting his eyes, and Pablo appeared to be studying the weave of the carpet. It hit Moody that Pablo was embarrassed for him.

Is it that I'm too nice? said Moody.

Now Clara met his eye.

I don't think that's it, she said.

Moody turned toward the door.

You seem nice enough, said Pablo as Moody hurried past him.

Halfway back to his dorm, Moody came very close to being murdered by a bolt of lightning. Indeed, we were in the mood to see him killed, but it occurred to us that he hadn't found love yet, which meant that according to the terms laid out at the beginning of the narrative, he had to be allowed to live a bit longer—and so we nudged the lightning bolt twenty feet to Moody's left, where it slammed into, or rather through, a chipmunk, poor thing. Who now would provide for that former chipmunk's family?

Christ! said Moody, who'd never before been so close to so much electricity. It flashed in his mind that Bloke, during thunderstorms, used to hide under the couch.

That dog had good sense, Moody thought.

He reached the safety of his dorm and ascended to the floor on which he lived, if that is the right verb. He turned the corner into the common room and was stopped in his tracks—though of course he wasn't really making tracks on the carpet—by the sight of the most beautiful girl he'd ever seen. Her face was really something, on account of her extraordinarily assertive cheekbones and other striking features, like her eyes. Also, she was naked and was being taken from behind on the common-room couch.

Sorry, she said.

We'll be done soon, said the boy who was do-ing the taking.

Don't hurry on my account, said Moody.

Now he really did make tracks. He made them across the common room and up the hall to his room, whose door he'd never been so relieved to close behind him.

19

The girl on the couch was Amanda, of course. She'd survived another three years at the orphanage and now, luckily for us—otherwise we're not sure how we would stitch together the pieces of this novel—was attending Moody's college on a scholarship for arts-oriented orphan girls from the tundra. By now she was, as Moody had perceived, drop-dead gorgeous. The orphanage's headmaster had been the first in what was already a long line of men, plus a few women and, in one small town, an oversensitive child, who had lost their lives on the spot when Amanda walked by or even just stood there. A number of woodland creatures too had died this way. It wasn't just Amanda's magnificent cheekbones or her you-gotta-be-kidding-me figure or her eyes, which were intoxicating in a smoky, just-out-of-reach way; it was also the fact that every time she so much as lifted a finger, sex, or the idea thereof, came off her in waves, which were also particles.

The boy on the couch was named Ralph. He was the first even remotely interesting boy at college who'd dared to talk to Amanda. She liked that he was daring, liked that he was tall, liked the fact that now, in the common room, he was handing her an unfiltered postcoital cigarette, or, as she thought of it—this was her little joke—a postcolonial cigarette.

I suppose we should get dressed, Amanda said as she fumbled with her lighter. Her hands always shook after sex.

That guy who walked in, said Ralph. Did you see his face? We could use him.

What he meant, Amanda knew, was that they could use the guy's face in one of their performance-art pieces. These tended to be a bit extreme. Having unannounced sex on the common-room couch was, for Amanda and Ralph, small potatoes. An example of a big potato would be the time Ralph stood idly by while Amanda, in what was billed as an auxiliary role, drew a series of vertical lines on her face, in blood, using a razor. *Against*, Ralph had called the piece.

Now Amanda shrugged and said, I want pancakes.

Ralph took a drag on his cigarette. He blew smoke toward the ceiling and made a show of studying his dick. It was of two distinct hues and was, Amanda had repeatedly assured him, big. He wants me to say it again, she thought, but she didn't feel like it, so she didn't.

They got dressed and drove to the all-night diner at the edge of the City.

The usual? said their waitress. Her name was Bernadette, and her life, which we're not allowed to narrate because of a contractual dispute, was totally bizarre and fascinating.

20

I feel like I'm really onto something, said Chad to his shrink, Dr. Love.

Cubes? said Dr. Love.

Cubes, said Chad. They're just—I don't know. They're powerful. I haven't felt this way about anything I've made in a long, long time.

Dr. Love jotted something on his notepad.

I feel like I've been given something, but I'll probably fuck it up, said Chad.

Just the way you always do, said Dr. Love.

Yes, said Chad. Why would these cubes be the first thing I ever got right?

Then again, why not? said Dr. Love. And why even speak in terms of right and wrong? Why not just say, I'm doing the best I can?

Because I'm not, said Chad.

Dr. Love again put pen to paper. Then he seemed to study his loafers for a minute while the room filled with what Chad had come to think of as the Silence of Significance.

When the room was full to bursting, Dr. Love looked up and said, Tell me more about the cubes.

I've made six so far, said Chad. No, seven. Three of granite, two of glass, one of résumé paper, one of sandpaper. I don't plan ahead. I just use whatever material seems right at the time. Of course, having them all be the same shape gives the project a certain coherence. I find that freeing. I still get to choose the size of each cube and in some cases the color.

You are excited about this project, said Dr. Love.

Sure, said Chad.

Tell me, said Dr. Love. Do you feel you've fucked up any of the cubes you've made so far?

Chad hadn't been entirely pleased with the first of the two glass cubes. One of its panels had for some reason clouded over in a way he hadn't intended. So that wasn't great, but to say he'd fucked it up would have been too strong.

No, Chad said, and he realized that his face felt as though it were smiling, which it was.

Well, then, said Dr. Love.

21

Lo! It's time for Moody to graduate from college and find a job. If that seems abrupt, well, it seemed abrupt to Moody too.

Don't think in terms of a job, said Moody's father one evening over the phone. Think in terms of a career.

I'm thinking in terms of a life, Dad, said Moody.

That's absolutely right, honey, said Moody's mother. But you don't want to spend your life worrying about money. And the only way to keep from having to worry about money is to start earning some. Or you could marry a rich widow.

Ha! said Moody's father.

Moody didn't know any rich widows, so it looked as if he was going to have to get a job. But what sort of work could a newly minted bachelor of arts who'd studied subjects like anthropology and ancient literature—subjects that were deeply enriching perhaps but were unconnected to any obviously marketable skill—get? Moody wanted, vaguely, to change the world for the better. Failing that, he at least wanted to avoid changing it for the worse. Or, if even that were too much to ask, he decided he would settle for a job that wouldn't adversely affect his own character. If it was true—and young Moody felt certain it was—that commerce tended to pollute not only rivers and streams and air but also the souls, or their secular equivalents, of the people who engaged in it, then it was of paramount importance that Moody avoid doing anything too commercial. On the other hand, a lot of people who did nonprofit work struck Moody as being, deep down, despite all their energy and commitment, simply depressed. So he was leery of associating too closely with that crowd too.

Basically—though he wouldn't have put it this way—Moody resented having to go out and become part of the world. He preferred to be a world unto himself. He wanted to fall in love, of course, but otherwise he was happy to think his thoughts and feel his feelings and be impressed by his impressions. He worried that a job would cut into the time he allocated to these internal activities.

Nevertheless, on the eve of his graduation, Moody did land a job: he would be delivering coffee beans for a gourmet coffee roaster in the City. It wasn't a job that was likely to lead him by any direct route to the sort of career his father might want for him, but, hey, a job was a job, and this, being a job, was a job. Besides, Moody liked coffee a lot, and although the job didn't pay very well, it did come with a perk: free coffee.

The next day, at the graduation ceremony— an ending if ever there was one, though it was Orwellianly dubbed a commencement—Moody found himself seated next to the astonishingly beautiful girl he'd seen, an indeterminate time before, doing the deed on the common-room couch. He'd since learned that she was an artist, a fact that only heightened her already tall allure. Never before had

Moody been as near as he now was to those famous cheekbones, and, under their sway, he had a hard time concentrating on the commencement speech. The speaker was a career diplomat who was saying bland things about a new era of ballots, not bullets, gain, not guns, whores, not wars—or no, Moody must have misheard that part. In any case, Amanda— that was her name, Moody remembered—now leaned very close to him and whispered, I think I heard you playing the piano the other night.

At this, it is our duty to report, Moody just about had an orgasm inside his rented gown. After all, Amanda was hands down the most beautiful woman on campus; she was probably one of the ten or twelve most beautiful women of all time; she was certainly at this moment far more beautiful than whatever was left of Helen of Troy. An associate dean had dropped dead at the sight of her (Amanda) in her graduation gown just half an hour ago. And this amazing woman, this Amanda, had noticed mere Moody? And paid attention to his piano playing?

You did? he whispered back, thinking that she was probably making fun of him, though he wasn't sure in exactly what way.

I think it was you, Amanda said, though in truth she had no doubt about the matter, for on Ralph's instructions she had trailed Moody to the music building.

I was walking through the music building, Amanda said, when I heard something cool, something improvised. I glanced into the room. It was either you or, like, your twin brother.

Play it cool, Moody told himself. Remember, beautiful girls are always whispering praise in your ear during public ceremonies. Happens all the time. Bit annoying, really.

I have two brothers, he said, but none of us are twins. And I'm the only one who plays piano.

Ralph and I need a musician for an event we're doing, Amanda said. Any interest?

Ah, Moody thought. Ralph. That tall guy he'd often seen Amanda with on campus—the guy from the common-room couch. Arrogant and artsy, almost a movie star in terms of the way he looked, he was a million times cooler than Moody was.

Sure, maybe, Moody said. I mean, it depends.

Call me, said Amanda, and she handed him a piece of paper with her name and phone number scrawled on it.

Will do, said Moody, and he wiped a bead of sweat from his brow.

Cute kid, thought Amanda. Could stand to relax, though.

Moody turned his attention back to the stage, from which the diplomat was urging the audience to consider the problem of recalcitrant minor states.

Just bomb them, Moody would have told the diplomat had the opportunity arisen. That's what you'll do anyway.

22

Moody's best friend from college, the son of a cabdriver with a gambling habit and a social worker with a cabdriver habit, told Moody he should wait a few days before calling Amanda. One didn't want to appear desperate, the friend said. One didn't even want to appear especially interested.

But I am interested, Moody said.

Moody, his friend said. It's a game, son.

It had never before occurred to Moody that love, or the pursuit thereof, might be a game—but now that he thought of it, it was true that there were winners and losers in love, which meant that it had to be a game or else some other kind of contest, like maybe a war.

So Moody didn't call Amanda just yet. In the meantime, he spent his mornings packing up orders of coffee beans and his afternoons driving a delivery van around the City to take those orders to the coffee shops and restaurants that had requested them. It was physically demanding work, everything except the driving, and at the end of the day Moody was not only bone tired but also muscle tired and perhaps even fat tired. He would come home to his rented room and heat two cans of soup and eat them both, or their contents. Then he would collapse into bed. Never before had he slept so well, nor would he ever sleep so well again.

One evening when he could stand waiting no longer, Moody dialed the number Amanda had given him. She answered on the third ring.

Hi, said Moody. It's Moody, the piano player. I—

Glad you called, said Amanda. Can you meet us at the village coffee shop in an hour?

Sure, Moody said.

What should I wear? he wondered after he got off the phone. All his clothing was mortifyingly un-artistic. It may even have been anti-artistic. He did at least have jeans, like anyone else. So, jeans then. And sneakers. And a T-shirt. Okay, that was settled. Whew!

He found Amanda and Ralph at a table on the patio at the back of the coffee shop. Ralph rose and shook Moody's hand and introduced himself. The tall fellow's jeans and T-shirt were tighter than Moody's, he wore not sneakers but combat boots, his hair was sort of slicked back, and he didn't re-move his sunglasses. Moody didn't even own a pair of sunglasses.

Amanda says you play a mean piano, Ralph said once they were all seated.

Moody looked at Amanda, who was despair-inducingly gorgeous in cutoff shorts and a tank top and who now very efficiently pulled her hair into a loose knot and said, Moody's perfect.

I'm sure I'm not perfect, Moody said.

Yes, you are, said Amanda.

You are, said Ralph.

They both looked at Moody as though to say, Deny it. Deny that you are perfect!

We're doing a project, said Ralph, splaying

the fingers of each hand upon the table, palms down. A project about the human face. It's called *Faces*. Note the plural. It combines photographs, sculpture, video, and one actual face. Hers.

He jerked a thumb at Amanda's face.

Amanda, Ralph continued, says your music is perfect for this project. It's off-kilter, ramshackle, a bit spare, maybe even a little off-putting. Essentially it is failed music. It fails at being what music should never have been asked to be in the first place, sort of the way the human face fails to be anything other than what it has always been. In other words, your music is a triumph, though not perhaps a deliberate one. We want you to perform at our opening. It's at Gallery Five in a few weeks. Yes or no?

Amanda's knee pressed against Moody's under the table.

Moody cleared his throat and said, I haven't done a lot of—

Doesn't matter, said Amanda. You're perfect.

No, you are, Moody said to Amanda in the silent voice that could be heard only inside his skull, where it was very loud. And it was true: look wheresoe'er one might, one's gaze came to rest upon a part of Amanda that was perfectly formed. Her neck, for instance, of which Moody had an unobstructed view now that her hair was up, was like an exhibit demonstrating what a neck was supposed to look like. Nor was the stimulation merely visual, for Moody felt approximately a hundred volts of direct current (as opposed to alternating current, which is the basis of attraction between people who are not just moody but bipolar) passing from Amanda's knee into his own.

All right, he said. I'll do it.

Great, said Ralph while Amanda flashed Moody a smile and, however, withdrew her knee.

When exactly is this happening? said Moody. He'd always gotten horribly nervous if he was going to play the piano in front of other people. He hadn't done it since high school, and then only twice, at recitals his teacher had guilt-tripped him into taking part in. You have a gift, she'd told him. You have an obligation to share it.

What if I don't feel like it? he'd said—words he was ashamed to recall now.

Third Saturday of next month, said Amanda.

Oh, too bad, said Moody, feeling suddenly sly and attractive. I'm giving a recital overseas that weekend.

Ralph and Amanda looked blankly at him.

Just kidding, Moody said. I can do it.

Good, said Ralph, and he brushed Amanda's face with the back of his hand. Shall we adjourn?

I'll call you soon, Amanda said to Moody as Ralph caressed the back of her neck. Moody said okay and then rose and left. At the edge of the patio he glanced back. Ralph and Amanda were French-kissing, and Ralph had a hand inside Amanda's tank top. Moody felt like a fool, even if he had just been asked to join, or at least accompany, some kind of avant-garde, if indeed that was what Amanda and Ralph were.

At home, Moody looked for, and found, the

loneliest, most dispiriting form of love, the kind a person finds all by him- or herself.

23

Moody didn't know where else to go to practice his improvisations except the music building on the campus of the college from which he'd just graduated. He took his old student identity card with him in case anyone stopped him, but no one did. He began going now every second or third night after work. Walking up to the music building's third floor, where the practice rooms were, he would imagine that he was following in the footsteps of the nineteenth-century composers about whom he'd had such romantic ideas in high school. Just as they had spun melodies out of thin air at the behest of some nobleman or muse, so now was Moody trying to deepen an improvisatory groove at the request of the most beautiful woman he'd ever seen. It wasn't exactly the same thing, but times had changed.

Moody had never given much thought to his improvisations. He didn't even think of them as improvisations, not quite. He messed around, was how he thought of it. He'd taken a jazz theory course during his junior year at the college with the idea that it might improve his life as a music listener, not as a pianist. To his surprise, the course had done wonders for his playing, albeit minor wonders.

Tonight, Moody was working at making his pianistic ramblings more melodic than they'd hitherto been. And yet, he thought, if his music became more melodic, it might be less pleasing to Amanda and Ralph, who wanted him to play in a way that was off-kilter and a bit off-putting. Indeed, Ralph had said, they wanted his music to fail—to succeed at failing, was how Moody thought of it, which was not the same thing as failing at succeeding.

The faint orange glow of the dying day filtered through the practice-room window and came to rest on the keys at the treble end of the piano. The name of the art project was *Faces*. Moody pictured Amanda's face. All that beauty, etc., plus the faint scars from that controversial performance she and Ralph had staged a couple of years earlier. It made Moody mad to think that Ralph had forced Amanda (for so he imagined the dynamic between them) to damage herself. Some men really were quite overbearing. Ralph was one of those men, Moody sensed, though in truth he didn't know much about the guy. For instance, he didn't know, nor would he have wanted to, that sometimes Ralph failed at sex—failed spectacularly—and that on those occasions he tended to weep and to beg Amanda to tell him that on most other occasions he was really, really good in the sack (or wherever).

And suddenly there it was, in Moody's fingers, a melody in three-quarter time, in B-flat major, a melody that was light and free and could never be weighed down by the likes of Ralph—a melody that, to Moody, somehow represented all that was best about Amanda, or all that he imagined might be best. And he didn't mean her face or anything else about her looks, for it was important to Moody to think in idealistic terms about any woman he was attracted to. (This may have been why so few of them went to bed with him.) Therefore he meant something about Amanda's essence, her inner goodness—her spirit. Mind you, he was not so dim a bulb as to fail to see that he only ever entertained exalted thoughts about the spirits of women whose earthly forms he found compelling. Oh well, he figured; no one's perfect.

The melody was pretty good, Moody thought as he played it again and again. But it needed to go somewhere, or rather, it needed to be prevented from going where it wanted to go. It needed to be pulled to the earth, like a bird that died while flying. Therein would lie the power of the melody, if it had any. Which was where a G minor chord at the bass end came in, Moody realized. Yes, that was it! To play the same B-flat melody over a G minor foundation, and then to return the whole thing to its major-key roots—he just might be onto something.

Just then, in the darkened sky above the music building, a shooting star blazed through its short life, but Moody, bent over the practice-room piano, and what with the opaque ceiling and all, didn't see it.

24

Amanda was smoking a cigarette on the rusty fire escape outside the kitchen window of her fourth-floor apartment in the City when a shooting star burned a hole in the sky overhead.

She saluted the shooting star with her cigarette. Thank you for your tribute, she said.

She knocked the ashes from the cigarette and watched them drift downward and flare out. Life had gotten boring of late. Not that being in college had been so terribly interesting, but since graduation she'd been spending altogether too much time in the company of ennui. It sat across from her at the breakfast table every morning. It labored alongside her at the auction house where she was a part-time receptionist. It even made threesomes of her couplings with Ralph. Am I alive? she would sometimes think.

The ennui would just sit there and say, Well? Are you?

Amanda's time-honored method of dispelling such thoughts was to do something she wasn't supposed to. But the problem with getting a studio-arts degree was learning that there was nothing you weren't supposed to do—or rather, to try to do something you thought you weren't supposed to do was exactly what you were supposed to do, which meant you shouldn't do it. Basically, unless you were a genius, there was no way out, no way to be anything that someone else hadn't already been.

The smoke rose in a straight line from the end of the nearly spent cigarette she held between two fingers. Maybe I should forget about myself and just read a book or something, she thought. She took a last drag, then flicked the butt of the cigarette onto the roof of the warehouse next door.

The phone rang. Amanda lifted the screen and climbed into the kitchen and picked up the receiver.

Yeah? she said.

Woman, said Ralph.

I saw a shooting star, said Amanda.

Ralph's breathing, or the sound of it, came through the line.

Woman, he said again.

Amanda held the phone away from her face while she lit another cigarette. Then she said, Not in the mood, Ralph.

Don't give me that kind of lip, little lady, Ralph said.

Amanda sighed. She'd come to find dreary and trite Ralph's little-lady, big-man game, a favorite of his. But it was best to avoid provoking Ralph when he was breathing heavily into the phone. And it wouldn't cost her much to play along—just a few minutes of a day she wasn't sure what to do with anyway.

So she said, I'll give you as much lip as I want, big man. What're you gonna do about it?

Ralph exhaled with pleasure into the phone.

25

Dr. Love was not looking forward to going to Chad's art opening. All his life he'd responded coldly to the visual arts, and although he'd never seen any of Chad's artwork, he'd heard enough about it to assume that he was unlikely to feel warmly toward it—especially because, ha ha, a cube was a cube was a cube, wasn't it?

Dr. Love drummed the fingers of his right hand on the worn-smooth wooden armrest of the old rocking recliner that was his chair of choice when seeing patients in his office. He frowned at his fingers, already the gnarled and baggy digits of an old man. He'd lately been plagued by the suspicion that his wife, Sylvia, might be having an affair with the chief financial officer of the housing-related nonprofit group of which she was the executive director. She spoke of him too often and a little too girlishly, was the thing. The chief financial officer, a thin, nervous man named James, seemed an unlikely womanizer, but one never knew, did one? Women, after all—even a woman as smart and capable and self-aware as Sylvia—were drawn like moths to the twin flames of money and power, and what did the phrase *chief financial officer* signify if not those two flames?

Sylvia'd been staying late at the office the past two months. That fact in itself would not have aroused Dr. Love's suspicion, for he knew the nonprofit group's annual report to the government agency from which it drew the lion's share of its funding was due in a few weeks. What aroused his suspicion was the glow Sylvia got when she mentioned James. James is so amazing, she would say. I don't know what I'd do without him. We'd be sunk if not for James. I'm meeting with James tomorrow evening, honey—don't wait up.

It was Thursday. Dr. Love frowned at his loafers, which needed polishing. Chad's art opening (and where was Chad? Dr. Love thought, checking his watch—late as usual!) was two days away. A Saturday night, and Dr. Love, instead of keeping an eye on his wife, was bound, out of the goodness and foolishness of his heart, to attend a client's foolheaded art opening. Cubes! Dr. Love had never heard of such a thing. And was it even professional of him to attend? He was skeptical toward the new theory that held that the traditional wall between therapist and client was a false construct that, though false, somehow managed to be real enough to damage both client and, to a lesser extent, therapist.

Things used to be simpler, Dr. Love thought, frowning.

There was a knock on the door. It was the tentative knock by which the artist Chad, né Jason Applethorn, announced that he was ready for Dr. Love to help him help himself.

Just eleven more years, Dr. Love thought, and he pictured his retirement, the house by the sea, the porch on which he would sit reading the newspaper with a pair of well-maintained loafers on his feet and a glass of bourbon in his hand and, in his ears, the sound, from inside the house, of Sylvia preparing his dinner, preferably pasta with red sauce. All of which amounted to little more than a dream, he knew, a dream he would gladly have admitted was standard and sexist and a bit boring—a dream that in any case could be snatched from him at any moment by a heart attack or a wifely act of betrayal or any of a number of other unwelcome developments.

Dr. Love sat up straighter in his rocking recliner and let his face die into the professional mask that he always carried at the ready.

Come in, he called in the direction of the door.

26

Friday, the day before Moody was to accompany Ralph and Amanda's performance of *Faces*, dawned like any other day: the earth in its relentless spinning brought once more into view the seemingly inexhaustible sun, and so on. Moody yawned. He wasn't a morning person, but even so, he enjoyed sleepily riding the elevated train to work, in his hand a paper cup of strong black coffee. How nice it was to transfer the coffee from cup to stomach, not directly of course, while watching the cityscape roll by outside the window. So many lives, he thought. So many buildings. Moody liked being part of the rush-hour flow of humanity—liked precisely the fact that although he was surrounded by other people, he wasn't socially obligated to exchange words with any of them. In short, it was nice to be alive.

And yet there was, underneath this feeling of the niceness of being alive, anxiety. For what was truly nice about this day was that it was a day on which Moody wouldn't be asked to do anything he wasn't already comfortable doing. Whereas tomorrow, Saturday, sometime after eight o'clock in the evening, at a place called (perhaps in reference to the number of fingers a pianist was expected to have on each hand) Gallery Five, Moody would seat himself at the keyboard of a piano he'd never played before—which mattered because no two pianos responded exactly alike to the touch—and

begin improvising. It was one thing to play an unfamiliar piano; it was another to do so before the
eyes and within range of the ears of a perhaps not
small number of people. (Though not certainly not
small, and anyway the number might shrink after
he started improvising—at which thought a lone
bead of sweat trickled down the back of Moody's
neck and was absorbed into the collar of his shirt.)

Clack clack clack! said the elevated train as
though it too were jittery about tomorrow night's
performance.

Moody's nerves settled once he got into the
flow of the workday. Render unto tomorrow what
is tomorrow's, he thought; today, pack up these
coffee beans. By the time he took his delivery van
out for his afternoon rounds, he was in fine spirits.
It was a nice day, after all, and he had no reason
not to believe he had a long life stretching ahead
of him. To top things off, there in the crosswalk in
front of him as he idled his van at a red light was,
coincidence of coincidences, none other than the
mind-blowing Amanda. Moody leaned his head
out the window to shout hello, but she hadn't seen
him and wouldn't hear him if he shouted, for she
was wearing headphones. The fashion that summer among young women in the City was to wear
flimsy clothing and formidable boots. Moody ap-
proved of this fashion, both in general and, now, in
particular. Just look at the way she's moving across
the street, Moody thought. It was a great way to
move, languid but quietly fierce. Amanda's gait
was all potential energy (or nearly all—she wasn't

just standing there, she was in fact moving, but her movements gave the impression that a lot more energy was at the ready than was being deployed in the service of crossing the street; but what the hell, she was young, she had better have more energy than that; in any case, what we mean is that her body was full of sex, more so than are most bodies, though all have at least a bit of it in them, thanks perhaps to some rare democratic impulse on the part of their creator, if there is such a being, which we doubt). The leather strap of Amanda's rustic-seeming over-the-shoulder bag pressed against her breastbone, which lived, as it should have, between her breasts, which were as much revealed as concealed by the gauzy material of her dress.

Her boots were implacable.

Moody was defenseless against Amanda, who wasn't even trying to attack him. He felt that he absolutely must get to know her better. What was she listening to on those headphones? Probably not piano music. She was an edgy girl, and although there was such a thing as edgy piano music, most people didn't know about it. Moody pictured her as a fan of punk, postpunk, neopunk, antiproto-quasipunk, or else rock. Electric guitar, in other words. Which was an instrument against which Moody had nothing in particular, but because he was in love with Amanda—no—because he wanted to be in love with her, he wanted her to be listening to piano music at this moment of their chance meeting, of which she was unaware.

Squirming with frustration as other pedestrians,

some of them staring in openmouthed wonder and one or two toppling inert to the pavement, blocked his view of Amanda's receding form, Moody tried to imagine where she might be going. The intersection at which he was stopped was, it occurred to him—damn, she was gone from view—just a few blocks from Gallery Five, where, a little more than twenty-four hours from now, Moody would play the piano while Amanda did... what? There'd been no rehearsals, no sneak previews, for Moody, of *Faces*. All he knew was that the performance would involve a bronze sculpture of Amanda's face. Be there at nine, was the only other thing she and Ralph had told him. Be there, and be ready to play.

The driver behind Moody honked his horn.

Moody's heart, or was it an intestine, gave a little flutter. He'd be there at nine, all right. But would he be ready?

27

Chad winced. He was in his studio, putting the finishing touches on the last of the cubes he would be presenting the following day at Gallery Five. It was almost midnight. Rain streaked the glass of the studio's high windows. Chad wished he didn't have to share the bill at Gallery Five with anyone, let alone a couple of performance/multimedia artists who'd just graduated from college. Amateurs! But that wasn't why he was wincing. Nor was he wincing because his back hurt, though it did.

The reason Chad was wincing was that he couldn't quite turn his mind's eye away from the expression he imagined must have come over the face of his former friend/lover at the moment when, hearing a strange noise, he looked up and saw that the train that had seconds before been traveling in the usual manner across the high trestle overhead was now, inconceivably but incontrovertibly, plummeting toward the spot to which he, the friend/lover, would a long moment later be nailed. By a train. It was unthinkable, really, but Chad couldn't stop thinking about it. The cube he was working on was made of actual, honest-to-goodness railroad rails that he'd obtained with the help of a friend of a friend of a friend. For all Chad knew, the doomed train that had doomed his former friend/lover might well at some point have ridden on these same rails.

The cube was hollow, an outline of a cube, a

line drawing made of steel. Chad sat upon his not entirely effective ergonomic seat. For two hours he'd been trying to weld together the rails whose juncture would form the cube's eighth and final corner. But he kept stopping and wincing instead and listening morosely to the rain upon the windows.

What would it feel like, he wondered, to have a train fall on one's head? Would it be like getting punched in the face—but all over one's body, all at the same time, and with much greater force? What might one's collarbone say when it was introduced to one's tailbone? The pain was unimaginable, yet somehow Chad had to get that level of pain into this last and most personal cube. All that pain plus the quite different pain of the loved ones, Chad among them, whom the deceased furniture designer had left behind.

If he couldn't express all that in cube form, Chad figured, he wasn't an artist. And if he wasn't an artist, he was just a file clerk at a low-cost health clinic. Which may not have been a bad thing to be, but Chad, poor fellow, had set his sights considerably higher. And now he was paying the price in beads of sweat.

Chad sweated a lot, and not only when, as now, he was welding steel to other steel, though this was indeed hot work. Maybe if he lost some weight he would sweat less, but on the other hand, if he was to have any hope of losing weight, he would have to start working out—an irredeemably sweaty business. It was a catch-22, he thought now as he leaned back in his ergonomic seat, pushed his industrial visor to the top of his head, and exhaled a puff of stale breath that spoke eloquently, though to no one, of the spaghetti with garlic, parmesan, and olive oil that had been his dinner. The drumming of the rain on the windows was oppressive. The angry droplets seemed to want to get in, like that crow in that book Chad vaguely remembered reading in high school. Was it a crow? Some dark bird in any case, and it can't have been a good omen that Chad's thoughts ran in that bird's direction now, the night before the art opening that was, although not a big deal in any cosmic sense, a very big deal to Chad.

Chad shook his head. Too much thinking, not enough welding.

He returned his visor to the safety position and set about finishing the final corner of the hollow cube that was to be, though he didn't know this yet, his first masterpiece.

28

With reluctant stride Dr. Love ascended the stairway out of the underground train system. Then, still moving without eagerness, he began walking on top of the ground, which was paved. All around him on the street were people his age or, mostly, younger. The women wore thin, short dresses and serious-looking boots; the men wore tight clothing in dark hues. At every turn Dr. Love's eye caught the glow of another cigarette butt as it was flicked, still burning, into the gutter. They were like miniature shooting stars, these butts, Dr. Love thought. Then he thought that he could do with a glass of bourbon.

Dr. Love had written the address of the art gallery on a scrap of paper and put it in the pocket of his loose brown trousers, about which he felt suddenly self-conscious. Ridiculous, he thought, a man my age worrying about his wardrobe. After all, he hadn't come to this unfamiliar neighborhood to appear stylish to the stylish people walking around in it. He was here for one reason only, and that was to do what he could to shore up the self-esteem of one of his many long-suffering clients. Which reminded him: it was time to think of something nice to say about Chad's cubes.

They're really something, he said to himself, practicing. They make a definite statement. Even though I don't know much about cubes, I can tell they're well made. I especially like the stone ones.

I've always liked stone. It reminds me of mountains. I like mountains.

Dr. Love shook his head. He didn't, in truth, care for mountains, not particularly. He was more of an ocean man. The ocean was moody and changeful, like a human being, whereas a mountain just stood there, doing nothing, like a god.

Dr. Love studied the numbers above the doors as he walked. Eleven, nine, seven... Ah, here it was: Gallery Five.

He lingered outside a moment. It was a nice night, not too hot, not too humid, not raining, not windy, no hail or sleet, nothing on fire. Gallery Five occupied the first floor of a four-story brick row home. It had a large plate-glass window. To the gallery's left was a brightly lit liquor store whose cashier sat behind bulletproof glass. To the right was a posh-looking sushi restaurant called, in fact, Poshi Sushi. The neighborhood was, a realtor would have said, in transition, which meant that the people whose modest incomes used to allow them to live there would have to find either a more boastful income or else another neighborhood in which to live. It was sad, Dr. Love thought.

Through the plate-glass window of the gallery Dr. Love saw a black upright piano and, above and to one side of it, a blank screen of the sort slides were projected onto. Toward the back of the room hung a red velvet curtain.

It was quarter to eight. The event was supposed to start at eight, but Chad had said the City's arts scene didn't have a punctual bone in its body.

A scene with a body, oh, well said, Dr. Love remembered thinking. Anyway, it was true that there didn't seem to be anyone in the gallery, though the door was ajar and a few people stood out front smoking cigarettes and talking loudly. Did art imitate life, or did life imitate art, or was everything just generally fucked up? a fat man with a loud voice wanted to know. Ha ha ha! he said.

Quarter to eight, thought Dr. Love. His wife was at this moment holed up in her nonprofit group's offices with James, the chief financial officer, cooking the books, as she'd said, for the group's grant application. Dr. Love frowned at the grimy sidewalk. *Cooking the books* seemed to him a suggestive turn of phrase. Though it would've been just as bad if she'd said they were *doing the numbers.*

Dr. Love rubbed the back of his neck. Across the street from the gallery was a bar. The thought of a glass of bourbon shone in Dr. Love's mind like a lighthouse beacon saying, Ahoy there, this way to safety. Dr. Love followed the beacon across the street and into the bar. It was a nice place, or at any rate it was dark and had candles. Dr. Love took a seat at the corner of the bar and ordered a glass of bourbon. The bartender brought it to him.

It was good.

The place wasn't crowded. A few middle-aged men drank alone at the bar, and some other people huddled at tables in the room's gloom. It occurred to Dr. Love that he too was a middle-aged man drinking alone at the bar. But the other men seemed sadder, more hunched over, more firmly ensconced in the world of drink. That word—*ensconced*—always made Dr. Love think of scones, though he knew there was no connection. In the back of the room a tall young man in tight clothing stood at the jukebox. Despite the dimness of the lighting and the fact that night was falling, the young man wore sunglasses. Dr. Love was just starting to chuckle at this when a song came on that had been a favorite of his and Sylvia's when they were youngish lovers. It was a song about a sailor who died at sea—*A thousand miles from you, my love*, the singer sang. *But I'm happy as I'm sinking, knowing that you'll think of me and cry.*

It wasn't a very good song, but still, Dr. Love mouthed the lyrics and, almost without noticing that he was doing so, moved his bourbon glass through the air in time to the music. *Knowing that you'll think of me and cry.* A tear leapt to one of his eyes. Embarrassed, he wiped it away.

Knowing that you'll—

Before he could get to *think*, Dr. Love was struck thoughtless by the sight of the most beautiful woman he'd ever seen. She'd been sitting at a table in the corner by the jukebox, apparently—he hadn't noticed her before—and had just stood up, causing heads throughout the bar to swivel. Dr. Love had borne mute witness to the external charms of no small number of striking women during the many years he'd resided in the City, which was famously a magnet that attracted whatever metal was the secret ingredient of feminine good looks. He'd even dallied with a looker or two decades ago during his brief heyday, and for that matter he'd seen attractive women in other cities too, and one or two in the countryside—but his eyes had never before been offered such fare as this. The woman's cheekbones, to take just one example, were epic, like something out of mythology.

Watching her glide or perhaps levitate toward the women's room, Dr. Love felt a sudden stabbing pain in or near his heart. It was a very sharp pain, not a good feeling at all, and it soon grew worse. Dr. Love clutched at his chest and gasped for air. With surprising calm he acknowledged to himself that he was having a heart attack.

But ah, no, thank goodness, it was just gas from the falafel sandwich he'd eaten too quickly before descending into the underground train system. Some portion of this gas now expelled itself from Dr. Love's rear end. He glanced furtively about. But of course no one was looking at him. Why look at a man in late middle age, even if you suspected him of being a public farter, when you could look instead at an abstract principle personified—one of the eternal forms come to life bodily here on our shabby earth, and in a dive bar no less?

The woman stepped into the ladies' room and was gone.

Dr. Love nodded with satisfaction as the bartender set bourbon number two in front of him. The bartender gestured with his head toward the ladies' room, his eyebrows arched.

Unbelievable, said the bartender. Chicks these days.

Tell me about it, said Dr. Love.

The bartender moved away along the bar, wiping it with his towel as he went, leaning into the work as though his life depended on it.

The woman came out of the bathroom and walked back over to the table in the corner and sat down. There was a man with her, Dr. Love discerned for the first time, a man or, no, a boy. Let's compromise and call him a young man, one who, Dr. Love could see even from across the dimly lighted room, was starstruck by the good or perhaps bad fortune of his company this evening. He was an altogether nondescript human being, this young man—every one of his features was a nonevent—and he seemed to know it, which meant that he also knew there was no earthly reason he should've been accompanied in this bar on this night by this woman to end all women.

Enjoy it, kid, Dr. Love wanted to say to the young man. It won't last.

Crush me with your love! shouted a rock singer just then from somewhere inside the jukebox. The tall young man in tight clothing turned from the jukebox and went over and slid a chair up next to the woman at the table in the corner and put his arm around her. Ah, thought Dr. Love. Of course. He's the one she's sleeping with—precisely because he's arrogant enough to think he deserves it. It won't last, buddy, Dr. Love wanted to tell this young man too. Perhaps Dr. Love wanted to say to all young men that it wouldn't last.

Moved by a sudden flood of half-formed images of his wife having fun without him, Dr. Love felt an urge to weep into his bourbon.

Throw me to your dogs! shouted the jukebox singer.

Dr. Love glanced at his watch. Twenty past eight. He drank the rest of his bourbon in a few aggressive swigs, paid his tab, stood up, took a last look at the woman, and went out the door to the street, where he stood for a moment shaking a bit of stiffness from the bad knee that afflicted him morning, noon, and night, poor man. We forgot to mention the knee until now, and we're not going to mention it again. It's up to you to remember it.

The sun had set. The street was more crowded than it had been, the crowd was younger, and Dr. Love was older, though by less than an hour. Many more people than before, perhaps two dozen, stood in front of the gallery, smoking or, in rare cases, not smoking. Squinting, Dr. Love pretended for a moment that the glow of the cigarettes was the glow of fireflies as seen in the scrubby woods that lined the shore of the lake upon which the twelve-year-old future Dr. Love and his childhood friends, some of whom were still alive today and even reported being happy, used to paddle canoes sometimes of a late-summer evening, long ago when the world was young.

One by one, the smokers threw down their fireflies and with the toe of a shoe extinguished their cancerous light. Into the gallery they went, along with the nonsmokers. Dr. Love followed them in.

29

You'll let me, right? Ralph was saying. No surprises?

Amanda cast an eye in the direction of the door to the men's room, behind which Moody'd gone to do whatever it was that men did in their rooms. Piss all over every surface that was anywhere near the toilet, she figured. Men were pigs.

Women were animals too, Amanda would be the first to admit, but they weren't pigs. What animal they were was harder to say and may have varied from case to case.

She studied Ralph's face. It was as angular as ever, and in his gray-green eyes she saw the usual hearty helping of grievance. Yet what did he have to feel aggrieved about? Amanda never refused Ralph anything he asked of her. She always figured she'd be able to say no to him someday, but no particular day, this day included, ever proved to be that day.

No surprises, she said, but what she was thinking was: Ralph, you're not half as interesting as you think you are.

Ralph smiled, squeezed her thigh under the barroom table, and said, That's my girl.

Amanda smiled at Moody, who was just then returning from the men's room.

We all set, Moodly-Mood? said Ralph, and he patted Amanda again on the thigh.

Yep, said Moody, looking at Amanda with what are known in literary circles as drowning eyes. Amanda doubted whether Moody'd ever had sex, or at least good sex. Maybe she would help him out sometime. He was a good kid. He just needed to loosen up a bit and start walking on the face of the earth instead of tiptoeing along a few inches above it.

The jukebox blared the first chords of a depraved-sounding folk-rock song about how much fun the apocalypse was going to be.

Moody said, This is the one I played for good luck.

I didn't know you liked this stuff, Amanda said.

Well, said Moody, I do.

I do too, said Amanda.

I don't, said Ralph, who then looked at his watch and said, It's time.

Fear was a sudden fist squeezing Amanda's heart, but not too hard.

She extended a hand over the barroom table and said, To art!

Ralph did and said the same.

Moody, as befit a piano player, held out both his hands—but he said To art! only once, which seemed to Amanda to be somehow profound, a statement that no matter how many hands pitched in, or how many fists, there could only ever be one art, and its name was Art, with a capital A. Amanda had already had two rum-and-cokes, one more than she usually had, which meant, she knew, that she was vulnerable to a false sense of profundity. But there were worse things to have a false sense of, as her father had sometimes told her while she stood waiting with chattering teeth to be dismissed after having carried yet another armful of wood.

The three friends, for lack of a better word, paid for their drinks and left the bar and, after looking both ways—which may as well be the moral of this story, for anyone who demands one: look both ways before you cross the street—crossed the street to the gallery.

30

It has been said, or at any rate it is about to be said, that if the totality of a person's mind is like a book, then his or her thoughts at any particular moment are like a page torn from that book.

Moody's mind as he crossed the threshold of Gallery Five was no different, except in his case the page was blank. He was physically aware of his physical attraction to Amanda's physical self, which had preceded his over the threshold, but he wasn't having any thoughts on this or any other subject. He wasn't even wondering if Amanda liked him, which was a thing he often wondered. Nor was he pondering the air of boredom she often exhibited in Ralph's company, sniffing at it to try to tell whether it was, on the one hand, a sign that she was indeed bored with Ralph or, on the other, a sign that boredom was a cool, artsy thing she and Ralph enjoyed doing together. Probably both, Moody figured, but not right now he didn't. No, the margins of Moody's mind as he stepped into the small, crowded art gallery were unlocatable, because the white space of his blank thoughts was no different from the white space that lay beyond the boundaries of those thoughts, which, again, he wasn't even having.

To be empty-minded was not, Moody knew from long-ago experience, the worst state of affairs for a person who was about to perform music in front of a roomful of people. But ah, look, he said to himself immediately upon having the foregoing thought: I am no longer empty-minded.

A shiver of pure animal nervousness rattled its way through Moody, starting in his teeth and exiting via his fingertips.

The gallery was dimly lighted and poorly ventilated. Moody plucked his striped button-down shirt away from his chest to let in what air there was. Had he chosen the right shirt? It was a little stodgy, perhaps, but his closet had nothing better to offer. He hoped his faded jeans and scuffed-up shoes would undercut any impression of stodginess.

Moody made his way through the crowd, which included a lot of attractive women—it was almost as if they didn't let women of less than striking appearance patronize the arts, which, if true, was antidemocratic in a way that Moody knew he shouldn't find exciting—until he found himself standing by the cheese table. He had a ready affection for all cheeses, hard or soft, sharp or mild, high-falutin' or barely falutin' at all. He loved them all equally, but that is not what we mean when we say that, before he died, a moody fellow named Moody Fellow found love. (What a letdown that would have been, eh?)

Moody eyed the manchego, trying to decide if it would suit his mood better or worse than the sharp cheddar beside it. He was saved from having to make this decision when a tall man standing near the piano in the center of the room began asking for the crowd's attention. The man was dressed from neck to ankle in black. Below his ankles were a pair of preternaturally white sneakers. Above his neck was his head.

Thank you all for coming out tonight to support the arts! he said into a microphone.

He said some other things too, and then, just like that, it was time for Moody to play the piano. His heart rate tripled as he went over and sat at the instrument, a studio upright with a tone that would be, he knew from the name of the manufacturer, a little too bright for his taste. Someone switched off the room's lights. Utter darkness now save for the dim orange of the streetlight slanting through the storefront window some twenty feet behind Moody. The middle of the keyboard was plunged into an inky blackness that was Moody's shadow. Shit, he thought, I can't see the keys. His pulse quickened even further, but he didn't experience heart failure or anything like that. No: to have so rapid a pulse at a time of stress was in fact a variety of heart success.

After a moment, the saving light of a slide projector blazed forth in the direction of the video screen that hung from the ceiling toward the back of the room. An amalgam of hot fear at having to start playing the piano any moment now and hot shame at having been so stupid as to forget that the keyboard would be sufficiently lighted by the slide projector flashed through Moody, making the back of his neck itch.

The word *FACES*, italicized and in all capital letters, appeared on the video screen and hung there quivering. Moody took a deep breath. Here we go, he thought.

The next thing that happened was that gasps ricocheted through the crowd as Amanda, wrapped from bosom to thigh in white gauze—she did not appear to be otherwise clothed—stepped into the light that poured like sudden, luminous milk from a spotlight five or six feet to the right of the piano. She looked like an angel or maybe a stunningly pretty ghost. The ghost/angel lifted her chin to Moody and nodded.

He began with a G minor chord in the baritone range. This was his favorite chord. It expressed not a weak sadness but a robust longing that could never be satisfied. Moody played the chord again, this time adding an F at the bass end. Amanda stood stock-still in the spotlight, a monumentally remote expression on her face. On the video screen appeared (and here Moody played the G minor chord again, this time with an E-flat in the bass— the descending bass line giving a sense of movement but not resolution) a series of black-and-white photographs of unsmiling faces of children from an earlier era, children who must have since grown up and died, children who, at least on the occasions here presented, had been very well dressed.

Had anyone in the gallery dropped a pin, and had Moody not been playing the piano, the collision of pin and floor would have been audible. Though why have a pin in one's hand in the first place at a moment like this? What we're trying to say is that there was, in the room, the sort of extremely focused hush that indicated that, for once, something special just might be happening. The dead, incidentally, hear precisely this hush and nothing else, certainly not piano music, at all hours of the day and night, and they never tire of it. We digress. Moody cycled through the chord progression again, this time deepening the bass notes by an octave. Faces of adults had replaced faces of children on the video screen. Like the children, the adults refused to smile, or maybe they weren't refusing—maybe no one had asked them to.

When Amanda bent and lifted out of the shadows at her feet a dark item of some kind—it was, Moody knew, a bronze mask depicting her face in a moment of ecstasy or sorrow—the crowd in the gallery held, by way of a cascade of individual efforts, its collective breath. When she rose and presented the mask to the audience, a few people near the gallery's door fell dead to the floor, such was the effect on them of seeing Amanda's face repeated. It was no worse a way to die than any other.

The instant Amanda lifted the bronze mask into the light, Moody launched into a more complicated, more strenuous version of the music he'd been improvising. Whereas before he'd been playing only a simple chord in the right hand and a lone bass note in the left, now he used his thumbs to bring out several internal voices, including one that sounded over and over a discordant note, F-sharp. He began to breathe more freely, and his shoulders and arms, hitherto too tense to allow him to produce a really melodic tone, loosened. He got that soaring feeling he sometimes got when he knew he was playing well. Even as he leaped into a suddenly glimpsed arpeggio—one technically demanding enough that he really should have kept his eyes on the keys—he risked a glance over the piano to where Amanda stood. At which point his breath jammed in his throat.

For there in the milky spotlight with Amanda was Ralph. He paced slowly around her, unwinding inch by inch the gauze that was her only claim to modesty. Ralph's claim was a loincloth. His entire pale body was coated in a reddish-orange powder. The expression on his face was frightening, the more so because of the red dust that made of his features a bloody mask, though bloody in a dry, slightly orange way.

They hadn't told Moody about this part of the performance. When enough gauze was pulled away for Amanda's left breast to pop into view, Moody let his hands fall from the keyboard. It was perfect, the breast; he regarded it solemnly. Then he peered at Amanda's face. She looked afraid—or no, that wasn't it. What it was was that she began to appear to be in the throes of, it had to be said, passion. Her face now resembled the bronze one she held before her.

Something happened then in Moody's inner life. Whatever it was, it caused him to jolt a forearm into the piano's keyboard, producing a snarl of sound so thick and jarring that Amanda and Ralph stopped what they were doing and stared at him, their faces registering a thing Moody hadn't known members of the avant-garde to be capable of: shock. For a moment the world seemed to tilt on its axis, which, in fact, is something that is always happening. Then a corner of Ralph's mouth curled ever so slightly upward, and he resumed slowly unveiling the body of his lover, who composed her features once more into a mask of ecstasy—or sorrow.

Seeing that the show would go on, Moody felt like dying, but instead he threw himself into an improvisation the likes of which he'd never before imagined. It sounded like Chopin trying to play Thelonious Monk after attending a Warren Zevon concert while on antianxiety medication that was backfiring. Meanwhile, Ralph began caressing Amanda's breasts and kissing her neck. Yeah! shouted someone in the audience. Amanda's nether regions were still wrapped in gauze—and then they weren't.

Another Yeah! and several No!s rang out as Ralph bent Amanda over and eased her to her knees. Oh no, Moody thought, where did the loincloth go? Amanda's palms splayed on the hardwood floor. Her face was full of sorrow now, definitely sorrow, Moody told himself as, sick to his stomach, he assaulted the high end of the keyboard. She doesn't love him, he said to himself as Ralph and Amanda, accompanied by a chorus of gasps from the audience, began—there was no other word for it—fucking.

The air in the gallery grew thick with audience discomfort or arousal or both. Or maybe it was simply the heat and humidity that were inevitable when a hundred living bodies, not to mention a few dead ones, were packed together in a modest-sized room. A third possibility was that public fucking was nothing new to the frequenters of the City's art openings, in which case perhaps the air was thick with boredom.

Moody, who'd been brought up to be polite, was vastly uncomfortable in this, a situation in which it was unclear what, if anything, would constitute polite behavior. Should he avert his eyes? Or would it be rude to ignore the performance? He compromised by keeping his eyes glued to the video screen, on which were projected a series of unsmiling farmers' faces from around the world. The sex that was being had, meanwhile, settled into a slow, steady rhythm. It seemed the very walls of the gallery expanded and contracted in time with the performers' movements. Moody had climbed down from the heights of his frenetic improvising and now played a quiet two-note trill in each hand, G and F, G and F, the notes wrapping themselves around each other, tumbling across each other, each trying to become what the other was. As the spectacle in the spotlight gathered intensity, Moody unconsciously increased the volume of his playing, his crescendo matching that of the lovers.

At length, Amanda cried out sharply, just once. Ralph finished a moment later and began to weep or to pretend to weep. In a late-breaking act of mercy, someone switched off the spotlight. The video screen was still lit up, and on it Moody was startled to see a projection of his own face—his face right now as he played the piano. Where was the camera? They hadn't told him about this, either. I look constipated, he thought. But my shirt collar looks good. At least I chose the right shirt.

Moody knew that *Faces* had come to an end, and he could barely see the keyboard in the light from the projector, but he kept on playing. He felt utterly alone, an astronaut left behind on the moon not because of a problem with the spaceship but because the others had simply forgotten about him and gone home. He still trilled two notes in each hand, wanting to suspend the moment, though he wasn't sure why: maybe to spare the audience for as long as possible the decision of whether to applaud the depraved spectacle they'd just witnessed, or maybe because he sensed that playing the piano while Amanda had sex with Ralph was as close as he was ever going to get to having sex with her himself—or no, we've decided, the reason Moody kept trilling his G and F and G and F was that he liked being in control of a roomful of people, every last one of whom had no choice but to sit or, in the case of the corpses, lie quietly in the dark until he decided he was done playing. Feeling expansive or perhaps slightly feverish, he artfully spun the long-running trills into the fabric of a new improvisation, one that centered on a dreamy melody that somehow married melancholy and a kind of smartass joviality. I ought to remember this and write it down, he thought.

Finally he brought the performance full circle, ending on a series of mournful G minor chords that dwindled away until the room, instead of being full of music, was full of having been full of music.

The lights went on. Polite applause rippled through the room. Amanda and Ralph were nowhere to be seen. The tall man who'd opened the proceedings reappeared with his microphone and said, Wasn't that something? We'll have a brief intermission now, ten minutes, fifteen at the most. Get some air, have a smoke, but don't, unless you hate art, leave. Still to come: the works of Chad.

Moody made his way to the cheese table. The weight of dread at the prospect of his first public piano performance in years had been lifted from his shoulders. In its place was a new, heavier weight, or no, it wasn't a weight, it was more as if he'd swallowed a knife: at any rate he was uncomfortable. He'd just been part of something that, had he been watching it from the audience, would almost certainly have upset him. Yet he'd helped it to happen, albeit sans foreknowledge. All of this was strange enough, but what was stranger was that Moody felt sort of good about the whole thing. And the fact that he felt good weighed on him or, if you prefer, cut his insides.

Nice work at the keys, said a haunted-looking man at Moody's elbow. The man was a member of a circus troupe whose performances were politically inflected without being humorless—not the easiest thing to pull off, especially if one was at the same time concentrating on juggling torches, a thing this man did five nights a week. He would twirl his flaming brands through the air and cry, To the greater glory of the abstraction known as the people! Often he wept while performing, and for this reason his stage name was Sad Man. He was dying of a rare liver disease, but he didn't know that yet. Moody didn't, and wouldn't ever, know any of this.

Thanks, said Moody.

Sad Man drifted off toward his grave. Moody sliced a bit of manchego and put it on a toasted piece of crusty bread. He had just bitten off half of this snack when he noticed a girl or woman hovering nearby. She really gave the impression that she was hovering. She didn't seem entirely real. Maybe it was that she was very small for an adult, if that was what she was, or maybe it was the outlandish way she was dressed. She wore exuberantly multicolored leggings, a short black skirt, a white button-down shirt, and, over the shirt, a red-and-green cardigan that ought to have clashed horribly with the leggings but somehow managed not to. On her feet were black lace-up boots of the sort that witches wore in movies. Between each of her eyes and the world was one-half of a pair of rimless spectacles. Her hair was dyed ruby red, and topping things off was a small black hat that, Moody intuited, would be more accurately referred to as a chapeau.

Hi, she said.

Moody swallowed his manchego and toast and said, Hi.

Some of what you played was really amazing, said the girl.

Smiling in what he hoped was a roguish way,

Moody said, Only some?

Yes, said the girl.

Moody's mind raced around and around the image of himself not being able to think of anything clever—anything at all—to say. Here we stand by the cheese table, was all he could think of, but even he knew enough not to say that.

At length he came out with, I like your chapeau.

That's because it's just right, said the girl.

Do you like cheese? said Moody.

Of course, said the girl.

Manchego is a good cheese, Moody said.

I know that, said the girl. But I could sort of go for a real meal.

Why was she telling him this? It was true, Moody thought as he eyed the young woman, who was slender to the point of barely existing, that she probably ought to eat a real meal. But he wasn't her life coach, so he said nothing.

The girl's eyes were laughing.

I mean, she said, that I was thinking of going somewhere else, right now, to get some food. You know, maybe there's a diner or something?

The girl brushed his arm with her hand. Her fingers were cold. Nevertheless, the heat of life shot through Moody at her touch. Looking at her delicate fingers, Moody—miracle of miracles—suddenly realized that she wanted him to go with her to get a bite to eat.

I'm sort of hungry too, he said.

The girl smiled and said, Let's go.

These words gave Moody such a thrill that, even though a voice in the back of his head was saying, Watch out, you don't know her, and even though he had wanted to see the second half of the art opening, and even though he vaguely remembered that he was a goner for Amanda, at least sort of, in a shallow way—even despite all these things, he said, All right, yes, why not, let's.

With that, Moody and the girl left Gallery Five, never to return.

31

Amanda saw them go. She was outside the gallery, smoking a postcolonial cigarette and amusing herself by classifying the glances audience members were throwing her way. They ran the gamut from disdainful to awestruck. Oh, thought Amanda, you poor, normal people with your normal, poor lives.

Moody's glance at Amanda as he left with the girl in the chapeau, who struck Amanda as being a bit spooky, may not have been a glance at all, for although his eyes flitted in her direction, he didn't seem to see her. He didn't acknowledge her, at any rate. That was okay with Amanda. If Moody was going to get some action, she was happy for him. He could use some action, and anyway he'd earned it by producing some excellent on-the-spot musical surprises. Amanda had never heard Moody play so well or, for that matter, so moodily. Watching him glide away up the street with the frail-looking girl, Amanda raised her cigarette in salute: Good job, Moody, you've earned your name.

She sighed. *Sexploits* was the title of the next performance-art piece Ralph wanted to do. He was hoping they'd be ready to unveil it at a big show in November that a friend of his was putting together. Tonight's exploit had been sort of a scaled-back trial run. Amanda closed her eyes, pressed thumb and forefinger to the bridge of her nose. In her opinion, she and Ralph would do well to avoid becoming known in the art world as a pair of one-trick ponies. Then again, to make any kind of mark at all in the City's crowded art scene was a victory. One wouldn't want to be still struggling to break in at age forty or fifty or a hundred, like the guy who had the second half of tonight's show.

Okay, maybe he wasn't a hundred.

To be clear: it wasn't the case that Amanda didn't enjoy the things she let Ralph do to her in public. There was, to be sure, something clarifying about faking an orgasm in a spotlight in front of dozens of people who'd spent the past few minutes studying your every movement or else studiously looking away. What exactly was clarified was, however, unclear, Amanda thought as she flicked her still-burning cigarette butt into the gutter and then lit another smoke. But there was at least a feeling that something might someday become clear.

Amanda had always liked brooding about her life. She liked poking and prodding the damned thing to see what it might be, liked hefting it to try to feel if it weighed anything. These activities made her feel comfortably separate from her life.

The reason Amanda liked feeling separate from her life was that if bad things happened in her life, she felt that they weren't necessarily happening to her.

She took another drag. People had been keeping their distance from her on the sidewalk, as though they were still uncomfortable with her nakedness, which was, after all, right there under the clothes she now wore. Amanda felt good, powerful, even fearsome. But she didn't want to scare anyone. All she wanted was... what?

Seriously, Amanda, what in the world do you want? she said to herself.

The audience started filing back into the gallery. Amanda ground her cigarette butt out against the pavement. She hoped Ralph had been able to calm down in the men's room. The sobbing had been too much, really.

At the threshold to the gallery, an older gentleman saw her face, gasped, and clutched his chest. Oh, god, not another one, Amanda thought. She covered her face with her hands and peeked between two fingers. A narrow escape: deprived of the sight of Amanda's face, the man pulled back from the brink of heart failure. His brow darkened by terror, he fled into the night.

Amanda took a seat in the remotest corner of the gallery and waited, along with the rest of the audience, which had thinned somewhat, for whatever it was that lay behind the red velvet curtain to be revealed.

32

Chad peered out from behind the curtain. Good, there was still an audience. A smaller one, yes, and not necessarily the right one—he worried that those who'd been driven away by the pornographic first act were precisely the people with whom his cubes might have resonated most powerfully, whereas those who'd stayed, hoping perhaps to see some more skin, would be disappointed. (The cube he'd made from a bat's hide wouldn't satisfy them.) Still, it was nice to see that his few friends who weren't dead or overseas or working the night shift were present. And there was Dr. Love, in the back corner, near the beautiful art-porn girl. Her face really was a work of art, and although her partner in depravity wasn't Chad's type, he was undeniably handsome—but that didn't mean *Faces* wasn't a completely vapid title for a piece of performance art that had left much to be desired, in Chad's opinion, and not desired in a sexual sense. Was that all those kids thought art was? The relentlessly predictable crossing of lines, the breaking for breaking's sake of taboos? At least the guy didn't hit her, Chad thought.

Then he thought: Never break a taboo because you want to be the one to break it. Break it because you want to see what the pieces look like.

He let the curtain fall back into place and turned and surveyed his cubes. He had put a lot of thought into their arrangement, using spatioartistic formulas and analytico-intuitive theories he'd read about in an arts magazine, but now the arrangement seemed all wrong. The trio of granite cubes was crowding the railroad-rail cube, causing the emptiness at the center of the latter to seem small or even cozy rather than sorrow-inducingly large and devoid of comfort. Just as troubling, the furry bat's-hide cube was lost now completely in shadow, as though it longed still to be the nocturnal creature from whose body it had been wrought—as though the cube were trying to remember what it had been like to be a bat—which was not at all the effect Chad had been going for.

Dismay seeped through the founder of the New Cubists like a poor substitute for blood. The exhibition was going to be a disaster.

But ah, no, Chad saw a moment later, the thing was, the bright overhead lights weren't on yet. That was why everything looked all wrong. Silly Chad, Chad thought. Every cube would be shown to be in its proper place once the proper lights were shining in the proper way. There was nothing to worry about—except whether his artwork had any merit.

Chad's hands were shaking. His feet felt as if they might be shaking too, though he couldn't see any movement down there, perhaps because of the combination of dim lighting and dark footwear. To please the memory of the former furniture designer, Chad had worn his black dress shoes, which his late companion had on several occasions loudly opined made him look like a man, as opposed to like a boy. But now Chad wished he'd worn the beat-up sneakers that, day in and day out, made him feel like the boy he knew himself still to be, really, on the inside. His mother would have understood. Chad didn't want to grow up, not ever, not even when he was an old man with a giant belly. Growing up, if he understood the concept correctly, meant accepting the world as it was.

I object! was one of the things Chad had tried to say with his cubes.

He'd tried to say other things too, but just now the gallery owner was motioning to him that the intermission was about to end—his cubes were about to be made public—and if he wanted to slink out into the back alley rather than be seen with his cubes, as he'd indicated earlier, now was the time.

Chad ran a finger along one of the top rails of the steel-rail cube. You are my prize, he wanted to say to it, but he felt awkward because the gallery owner was looking at him. So he didn't say anything.

Out the door into the back alley he went.

33

Dr. Love couldn't recall ever having witnessed anything so depraved, so disgusting. And yet in truth he'd found the whole thing rather stimulating. But also disgusting. And depraved, definitely depraved.

There she was, the degraded beauty, just a few seats to his right, clothed once again in the jeans and button-down shirt she'd been wearing in the bar across the street. Dr. Love could barely look at her, he felt so ashamed, but whether he felt ashamed for her or for himself was hard to say.

The guy who'd raped her, which wasn't the right verb but wasn't exactly the wrong one either, was nowhere in evidence. Nor did Dr. Love see any sign of Chad. He had no idea whether, in general, a sculptor was likely to attend his own art opening. If Dr. Love knew his client at all, the poor fellow was somewhere on the premises, perhaps in hiding, perhaps in disguise, perhaps wringing his hands in despair behind the locked door of the men's room.

The gallery owner, if that was who he was, stepped from behind the red velvet curtain and said a few words about Chad's art. Dr. Love's mind refused to focus on the words. He blamed the man's lackluster speaking style and his voice, which was like a gentle mist that quickly dissipated. In any case, his remarks were of short duration, the curtain was soon pulled aside, and there they were: Chad's cubes.

Dr. Love arose and moved with the rest of the audience toward the cubes. There were about a dozen of the things, each of them bathed in its own beam of light, each fully occupying the space allotted to it within the back half of the gallery. There was something immediately compelling about the cubes, Dr. Love sensed. What they compelled a person to do was look at them.

Each cube had its own personality, or cubality. Take, for instance, the three small granite cubes that clustered together in three pools of light that overlapped like parts of a Venn diagram. They seemed almost to be gossiping, these cubes, but not in a malicious way. They had a kind of stony warmth to them that Dr. Love wouldn't have thought Chad could find within himself or for that matter within nature. People were endlessly surprising, though, was a thing Dr. Love had learned over the years. Even one's wife of several decades could surprise one. The thought sent a little tremor of anxiety down his spine and into his tailbone.

The stunning, oversexed art girl was circling slowly round a cube made of résumé paper that hung by a string from the ceiling. Something about the way it hung gave one the impression that it had hanged itself, Dr. Love thought—but perhaps that impression came less from the cube and more from the sadness under the eyes of the great beauty, who was clearly a lost soul and an angry one. Her anger just might save her, he knew, from whatever internal or external forces were pressing in upon her or out from within her. But he also knew something she, being young, most likely didn't: anger was not the easiest tool to keep control of.

What would this fierce young woman be made of if she were a cube? Dr. Love thought, and then he wondered why he was having a strange thought like that. I myself, he thought, would be a glass cube filled with bourbon, pipe smoke, and useless knowledge.

Happy with that image, Dr. Love made his way along the perimeter of the room. He encountered a rustic wooden cube that spoke to him of the joys of honest labor, such as they were; a tiny, furry cube that seemed lost in a gloom of its own devising; and, at the center of the room, a three-foot-high cube that was really just an outline of a cube, a metal frame in the shape of a cube. This frame-cube appeared to be made of railroad rails. That was all the information Dr. Love needed. Here, he knew, was a monument to Chad's former friend/lover, the one who'd been killed by a falling train. He'd been a cheerful fellow and was still the most important person in the artist's mental life aside from, first, his mother, who'd died longer ago and less spectacularly (she had merely fallen; nothing had fallen on her), and, second, himself, i.e., Chad.

When Chad had first started seeing Dr. Love, he hadn't even ranked himself in his own top five in terms of his mental life. So there'd been progress.

Dr. Love stood and admired the railroad-rail cube. An aching sadness came off the thing in waves or, if not in waves, then in one steady, even transmission. The key to the sadness, Dr. Love correctly perceived, was the emptiness at the cube's center, an emptiness that, being air, was the same emptiness that flowed into and out of the lungs of the viewer, thus connecting the viewer with the pain of the artist's loss, a pain that was palpable, Dr. Love suspected, even to viewers who couldn't have known its source.

But there was more to the cube than what wasn't there. There was, additionally, steel. So unforgivingly straight and true were the railroad rails, and so cold and indifferent the light that glinted off them, that they struck Dr. Love as being somehow genuinely evil. He drew back as though he'd been slapped.

He hadn't known art could be so exhilarating. He looked around to see whether anyone else had been struck by the power of this railroad-rail cube. The answer was yes. Almost the entire audience had by now made a circuit of the room and come to a halt in the vicinity of this one cube.

Wow, said a gray-haired man to Dr. Love's left who was staring at the cube with tears in his eyes.

Yeah, said a fashionably dressed young woman to Dr. Love's right.

Others nodded their heads or murmured in agreement.

Dr. Love drifted off into a morbid fantasy about walking in on his wife and her chief financial officer as they were engaged in the most ancient of personal misdeeds, then dragging them both by their hair to the nearest set of railroad tracks and tying them down together to await the weight of the judgment against them. He recognized that the fantasy was unhealthy.

Brushing his elbow now and sending him into a different kind of reverie was the elbow of the beautiful sex/art girl. It had been an accident, he saw, the contact. Still, he would treasure the memory of it until the day he died, if not longer. Her face was turned away from Dr. Love's and toward that of her partner in depravity, who'd reappeared at some point. His hair was wet, a fact Dr. Love found disturbing.

These cubes are the next big thing, Dr. Love heard the wet-haired fellow say.

Definitely, said the girl.

We have to talk to this guy, said the fellow.

Definitely, said the girl.

Dr. Love experienced a surge of vicarious glee. Were these two talking about the works of—Chad? The bedraggled middle-aged client whose inner life, Dr. Love happened to know, contained about as much warmth and light as a coffin?

Good for you, Chad, thought Dr. Love, but at the same time he felt a twinge of something this particular client had never before inspired in him: envy.

Dr. Love shook his head, perhaps seeking to clear it. It didn't work. What he needed was to be alone for a few minutes, alone with his pipe and tobacco. There was an exit sign at the back of the room. Moved as though by the unseen hand of some hidden plural narrator, Dr. Love, rather than going out the front door of the gallery to smoke on the street, glided toward the exit sign at the back and then underneath it, out the back door and into the back alley.

34

What's your name? said Moody to the girl with the chapeau as, in the brightly lit interior of a noodle house that overlooked a desolate train yard, they bent over steaming bowls of noodles in broth.

I'm Kate, she said. What are you?

Moody, said Moody.

But what's your name?

That is my name, said Moody. Moody Fellow.

Kate grinned and said, It's perfect. The perfect name for you.

Most people don't think so, Moody said, though he had no idea whether that was true. He didn't know what most people thought about anything.

Is it your stage name? she said.

Moody shook his head.

I like it, said Kate. Tell me, Moody Fellow, what do you do when you're not playing moody piano music while other people have sex?

Moody blanched, or felt as though he must be blanching. What a first impression to have made.

I deliver coffee beans, he said.

First job after college? Kate said.

Moody nodded. He slurped some broth, eyes down. One of his legs kept shaking the way it sometimes did when he was playing the piano if he knew there was anyone listening.

What about you? he said.

Kate said, Oh..., then adjusted her chapeau

while looking into the mirrored wall by the booth in which they sat. My family are all dead, for starters, she said.

Moody let fall the noodle he'd been chopsticking toward his mouth.

It happened a long time ago, said Kate. One learns to cope. One learns even to love death. Aside from that, let's see. I work at a stationery shop two days a week and am otherwise unemployed, but I never get bored. I don't believe in boredom.

Is she crazy? Moody thought.

What happened to them? he said. If I may ask.

My father, she said, suffocated when he fell into a silo full of sugar at the soda-pop factory where he worked. Every attempt to climb out of the sugar only caused him to sink deeper, until he was completely submerged, as though in granulated quicksand. It was three days before they found him.

Moody gulped.

My mother died a week later of the cancer that had been slowly killing her for two years, Kate said. It began in a kidney and ended up in both lungs. My father had been staying up at night watching over her, because toward the end she had so much trouble breathing, he was afraid she would suffocate during the night. So he kept himself awake and watched her breathe while she slept. Mornings, he went off to work. I think he must've fallen asleep on his feet and tumbled into the sugar.

I'm so sor—

My two brothers, Kate said, died in a car

crash. They were both driving. They crashed into each other at the main intersection in town, maybe on purpose. They died within seconds of each other in the ambulance on the way to the hospital.

Kate was full of rage, Moody realized. He had no idea whether the things she was saying were true—no idea if these events were the source of her anger—but he did see that her off-the-wall persona was a defense against her rage, a way of trying to outrun it or (and here Moody remembered his initial impression of her) float away from it.

She was adjusting her chapeau again.

I don't know what to say, Moody said.

Kate smiled. Our dog mauled our cat, she said. That was the last bad thing that happened. Or, well, then the dog died of remorse. So now I'm all alone in the world, just like everyone else.

My dog died too, said Moody.

How? said Kate.

Old age, said Moody. She had a good life.

Oh, said Kate.

Moody was embarrassed. This girl knew so much more than he did about what the world could do to a person. At least, if she wasn't making all that stuff up, she did. And he didn't think she was making it up, though he couldn't have said why he didn't think so. Maybe it was just that he wanted her to be telling the truth, both because it would be better to date a woman who told the truth (yes, Moody realized they were about to start dating, had already started dating) and because he found the idea of so much death and loss quite attractive. That sounds horrible and strange, but it isn't really, not if you look at it the right way. Moody, an inexperienced young man, hungered for things that were big and real, that's all. He was ready, or thought he was, to begin shouldering a man's share of the world's weight.

Listen, Moody said, do you want to go bowling or something?

Kate shrugged.

We can do that if that's what you want to do, she said.

What do you want to do? said Moody.

There's this new film from overseas, she said.

On the way to the movie theater, Moody kissed her, surprising himself but not Kate, who didn't know him well enough to be surprised. The kiss was a shy one, and Moody immediately began worrying that maybe it hadn't been adequately exciting for this strange young woman who had lost so much, if indeed that were true, and whose desire for intensely life-affirming activities like passionate kissing was presumably quite fierce. (Later he would learn that in fact Kate didn't like kissing, not particularly. She thought it was messy and a cliché.)

They came to a bridge that crossed over the rail yard that sprawled below the noodle house. Moody liked the yard, liked how peaceful it was. It was full of nighttime trains that weren't going anywhere.

When Kate looked at the yard, she saw something different. She saw the next morning's trains getting ready to move.

35

Three weeks later, Moody and Kate moved together into a new apartment. It wasn't new in the sense of being newly constructed or even newly renovated; what was new about it was that neither occupant had lived there before. Moody had at first suggested that he simply take up residence with Kate in the apartment she'd been living in for the past two years, but she'd disagreed. It was important, she said, that the love that had sprung up between them (for yes, this had happened) be planted in virgin soil. Or, if their love turned out to be the kind that was also a war, then it should be fought on neutral ground, she said.

The apartment was sunny, at least on sunny days, and in all kinds of weather it was in need of repair. The bathroom sink couldn't be shut off entirely. The linoleum of the kitchen floor was mysteriously browned in patches. The floors of the entire apartment slanted away from the building's outer walls; if you set a tennis ball on the floor, it rolled. The windows, though new and double-paned, didn't quite fit their frames. Only about two-thirds of the electrical sockets had electricity behind them. There was a pile of rusty nails in the oven.

Moody loved the place. It was gritty but not too gritty, authentic yet somehow not quite real. But what he loved most about his new home was that Kate was living there with him. It meant, he supposed, that she truly loved him—he'd finally found love!—and therefore his life was not only complete but also, though he wasn't yet aware of this, almost over. So that was nice, as was the fact that Kate added a handful of distinctly womanly touches to the apartment's interior: she installed a decorative shower curtain, for instance, and every Friday she bought tulips or daisies or representatives of some other flower species and put them and some water in a vase that she then set upon the kitchen table, which slanted because the floor slanted. The floor slanted because it was old.

Directly below the apartment was a cheese shop. This pleased Moody to no end. He befriended the shop's owner and learned the word *artisanal*. It meant good but expensive.

Having a girlfriend was artisanal, Moody found. Kate liked to be taken out to dinner and subsequently to dessert. It was awfully nice to have a girlfriend to dine with, but at the same time, Moody didn't make a lot of money delivering coffee beans. Luckily, Kate also liked to stay in and cook. Her signature dish was one she called shrimp à la wow.

Moody and Kate were at first a bit drunk on sex, as often happens in such cases. Like other forms of drunkenness, this one can be quite enjoyable while it lasts. Of course, any two people are likely to have different approaches to getting drunk. So it was with Moody and Kate in bed. Moody wanted the world to end in an explosion of sexual abandon, whereas Kate, ever the more forward-looking of the pair, thought that the world ought to continue so they could have sex again tomorrow. The important thing was that they each had a clear philosophy and stuck to it.

They had other things in common too. Chief among them were: a) smarts; b) moodiness; c) an unusual and, Dr. Love might have said, dangerous ability to hide that moodiness from view; and d) enthusiasm for the arts. Neither of them was enthusiastic about every single art form—Moody was mostly indifferent to paintings, for instance, and Kate refused to read anything labeled a memoir—but still, there was enough overlap in their enthusiasms that they were able, most evenings, to decide, without arguing, which of the City's artistic events to attend, if any, and which if any to avoid. (Their relationship hadn't yet matured or subsided to the point where it would have occurred to them to attend separate events, each according to his or her whim.)

Among the events they attended were a number of readings by authors peddling their books. Moody discovered to his amazement that he was capable of liking poetry. Sure, some of it was so pretentious or obfuscatory as to seem to have been written for the express purpose of stirring hostility in the heart of the reader or listener. But other poems were quite pleasing to listen to or to read or even, though this was rarer, to think about. There were, it turned out, certain ideas or images that kicked you in the solar plexus if worded in just the right way.

Poets are ninjas of the mind, thought Moody, who was no poet.

As was mentioned, Kate had a job at a stationery shop. One way in which her job resembled Moody's was that it didn't pay very well. As a result, the couple developed a special fondness for artistic events that were free. Many of these—for instance, an outdoor one-act play they attended that had no plot, no theme, no compelling characters, and dialogue that was strikingly dissimilar to human speech, all of which might have been forgiven on a less rainy night—were not very good. So they started going to free lectures instead, figuring they would at least learn something. Moody didn't know what it said about the two of them that a lecture about legislative politics in some faraway land could inspire them to ascend afterward to new heights in bed. Whatever it said, it was wonderful to have found a kindred spirit.

For that was the key to happiness, Moody understood for the first time in his two-plus decades as a living being. Find a kindred spirit and you can be happy no matter your circumstances—unless maybe one of you is detained by your country's secret police or gets a terrible illness or has an affair or if you both lose your jobs or one or both of you get hit by a car, bus, truck, train, or fast-moving bicycle or else you just get really depressed, any of which can befall anyone at almost any time, without warning. Find, however, no such spiritual relative, and all the money in the world, plus all the, say, coffee, can't save you from doom and gloom and sitting alone in your room—although admittedly those things happen to people in relationships too.

I should write a poem about my new insights into happiness, Moody told himself. He told Kate the same thing.

You're terrible with words, she said. Write a piece of music about it instead.

My true love knows me so well! Moody exulted.

He played the piano two or three times a week after hours in the basement of a church whose janitor he'd befriended. The janitor would let him in and would then stand by the piano listening to Moody's music and occasionally launching into a speech intended to convert Moody to his faith, which, he said, had saved him from darkness after he'd cut another man's eyelid in a knife fight.

There is only one way to be wiped clean of sin, the janitor would say, leaning on the piano and smiling at Moody's chord progressions.

Moody was struck by how janitorial was the janitor's metaphor for salvation. He wondered if the cheese-shop owner, had he been a man of religious conviction, would have spoken of believers' well-aged souls or even perhaps of humanity's moldy imperfection.

I'm not sure I agree with you, Moody would tell the janitor, and he would switch to a dissonant jazz chord.

Moody held no firm beliefs about ultimate matters. He believed in love and was against war and thought that when you died you were dead forever, which was one reason he was against war and in favor of love. But the name of the main reason he was in favor of love was Kate.

I love you, he said to her at least five times a week.

I love you too, she would say.

Moody wouldn't have minded if Kate had sometimes initiated these exchanges. *I love you too* was a nice thing to hear, but an out-of-the-blue *I love you* would've been like a grenade of love landing suddenly at his feet, Moody theorized. But oh well, he thought, one can't have everything.

And of course in the end one can't keep anything at all.

36

Fast-backward a month or two to the night of the art opening. Remember, Chad was hiding out in the back alley. Here now came Dr. Love, stepping into the alley to smoke his pipe. He lit the thing, puffed on it, looked around, was startled.

Hi, said Chad.

You scared me, said Dr. Love.

That was not my intention, said Chad.

Since when have you ever done what you intended? Dr. Love thought but did not say. Instead he puffed again on his pipe, leaned against the brick wall, and said, Your cubes are a hit.

You don't have to say that, said Chad, jamming his hands into the pockets of his beat-up sweatshirt.

I'm not saying it to be polite, said Dr. Love. And I'm not saying it because I'm your therapist. I'm saying it because it happens to be true. People love the one with the rails.

Chad froze. And—the other ones? he said.

Dr. Love smiled and told him that the other ones were well liked also.

Chad's shoulders slumped, and he half-collapsed against the wall, but Dr. Love could see that this was a good thing. It wasn't every day a therapist got to look on as years of tension evaporated from a client's body.

Thanks for telling me, said Chad. I was afraid it would be a disaster.

One mustn't be governed by fear, said Dr. Love.

Sorry about the opening act, said Chad. Crazy kids, right? No imagination.

Don't worry about it, said Dr. Love. In my line of work, you hear everything. Tonight it was more a matter of seeing everything.

I thought the kid on the piano was pretty good, Chad said.

Was he? said Dr. Love. I think he's in love with the girl. I saw the three of them before the show in the bar across the street. He must be into humiliation. I hope he has a good therapist.

A ragged wind swirled through the alley, brightening the embers in the bowl of Dr. Love's pipe. He wanted to ask Chad if making the railroad-rail cube had helped his wounds heal at all, but something stopped him. Perhaps it was the entwined odors of urine and garbage that greeted him each time he inhaled. A back alley was no place for a therapy session. Anyway, Dr. Love didn't hand out therapy for free.

How's your family? said Chad. I mean, if you have one?

If Dr. Love didn't answer right away, it was because, at least according to the old theories, it wasn't good for a client to know too much about his therapist. But for every old theory there were a dozen new ones, each of them at odds with the others and in many cases with itself. All of which made Dr. Love deeply weary.

I have a wife, he said, puffing on his pipe.

Kids? said Chad.

No kids, said Dr. Love.

At the core of the garbage smell in the alley was the very particular, very sharp fragrance that is loosed by rotting rinds of citrus fruits.

I like kids, said Chad. They pull you out of yourself.

Sylvia'd had two miscarriages in years gone by, each of them bringing to an end a pregnancy induced by Dr. Love, who at this moment very much wanted another glass of bourbon.

I almost forgot, said Dr. Love. I overheard the sex kids from the first act saying your cubes could be the next big thing.

Chad snorted. As if they would know, he said—but by the way he stood straighter and ran a hand through his hair, Dr. Love could tell he was pleased.

A rat scurried past them and crawled into a hole in the base of the wall opposite the gallery's back door. Dr. Love put his pipe and tobacco away in his jacket pocket. Then he stuck out his hand, and Chad shook it, and a few more words were exchanged—Congratulations, for instance, and See you Tuesday—and then with a wave of his hand Dr. Love stepped back inside the gallery. The cubes were still there, but all the people had gone. Dr. Love poked his head back out the door and said, Coast is clear.

I'll hang here a bit longer, said Chad.

Don't let the rats get you, said Dr. Love, and then with another wave he turned and walked through the gallery, out the front door, and up the street to the underground train, which he rode back to his neighborhood. At his stop he got off the train just as he usually would have, ascended the stairs in the normal way to the street, which looked like itself, and then walked to his home and up the stairs of the porch (his feet falling in precisely the same spots they always did) and through the front door into the living room, where his wife sat sobbing on the couch and would not meet his eye.

37

What did you do with my spoons? said Moody.

Kate looked up from the alternative fashion magazine she was reading and said, What?

My spoons, Moody said. Where are they?

I moved them, said Kate.

Where to? said Moody. Also, why?

They're right in front of you, said Kate.

Moody looked. Indeed, there they were, in a pint glass on the kitchen counter. He grabbed one, then took it and the bowl of cornflakes and milk that was in his other hand to the living room, where he sat down opposite Kate.

What have you got against the idea of a silverware drawer? said Moody, but even as he said it he thought, I can't believe I'm talking like this.

What have you got against being nice? said Kate, and though her smile was a bit chilly, there was warmth in her eyes. The rest of her expression was room temperature.

I was brought up to be nice, said Moody. So this is, like, my big rebellion.

He grinned the crooked grin he knew she liked.

Kate made her although-I-forgive-you-I-do-so-grudgingly face—she had a very talented face—and then said, Speaking of which, when do I get to meet your parents?

This weekend, said Moody.

It was true. That weekend the place where suburban subdivision met countryside became, in addition, the place where Kate met Moody's parents. The visit went well. Moody's mother liked Kate because she was smart; his father liked her because she didn't talk too much and was cute. Moody's brothers were away and so couldn't render an opinion. Kate liked Moody's parents because they were good people. And everybody except Moody liked Moody. All in all, it was a happy gathering.

The following weekend, Moody and Kate rode the bus to the point of land from which she had scattered her parents' ashes and, later, the ashes of her brothers. The point of land was on a rocky coast that was often shrouded in fog but was on this occasion bathed in a brilliant early-autumn sunshine. The air was crisp and good. The day of the parental scattering had been similar, Kate said.

So convenient that they died just a week apart, she joked grimly.

Moody made no reply. He'd learned pretty quickly that Kate needed to say things about her family from time to time and that for the most part she didn't need or want him to say anything in return. Four deaths in a five-person family were not a thing about which very much could usefully be said, was Kate's position on the matter. To Moody this not only made sense but also was a relief. He wouldn't have known what to say had he been expected to speak.

They walked atop the jumbled rocks until they came to the spot from which the ashes had been released into the waters. The sunlight leapt as though joyfully off the curved face of each small wave as it rose and then fell sighing onto the rocks. Kate told Moody that after she and her brothers had scattered their parents' ashes, they'd stood for a while in silence and that during that time a fishing boat had come chugging toward them along the coast. She'd half expected, she said, that the boat would pull up to where they were standing, and somehow, magically, their mother, free of cancer and not the least bit dead, would step ashore and smilingly announce that it was time for lunch. Their unsuffocated father would have been at the wheel of the boat, she said, grumbling about the tides or how the engine wasn't working right, and they would all have been together again and happy.

Or happyish, she added.

Silence, Moody knew, was expected of him, but it was such a nice day, and he was so glad that Kate was including him more and more in her life, that he had to swallow the urge to smile broadly and say something wildly optimistic about his and Kate's future together. He gazed as though pensively out over the water.

Will you do something for me? Kate said.

Moody nodded.

I want you to improvise some piano music that captures the character of this point of land, she said.

Okay, said Moody, though the idea made him nervous. He lifted her chapeau and kissed the top of her head. Her hair these days was lime green.

Moody closed his eyes and took in sharp

breaths of air through his nostrils in an effort to get to know the place better. Salt air, low-tide mud-rot, etc. What sort of music might evoke such impressions? Ultimately it depended on the weather, he decided. Today's was major-key weather, but that would not be this rocky point's dominant mode. He was going to have to mess around a bit at the church-basement piano.

Hours later, as their return bus snaked its traffic-slowed way through the City's outskirts, Moody saw through the bus window a giant cube made of wooden boards that had been nailed together and painted bright red. It stood about thirty feet high in an otherwise abandoned lot in a neighborhood that was nondescript or at any rate shall here go undescribed.

What is that thing? said Kate.

Looks like a cube, said Moody.

What's it for? said Kate.

Maybe it's—art? said Moody.

Looks like a barn to me, said Kate.

A barn in the City? said Moody. A barn with no door? A barn that is a cube?

The door must be on the other side, said Kate.

Art, said Moody.

Barn, said Kate.

One thing Moody liked about Kate was that although she herself was whimsical, in terms of both her fashion sense and her sense of how to spend, say, a Saturday afternoon—a mustards-of-the-world taste test had been a recent outing—she maintained an air of skepticism or even defiance toward other people's whimsy. That was why she needed to see the cube as a barn, he figured. Although then again, wouldn't a cube-shaped barn on a City street have been decidedly more whimsical than the giant, self-serious art object Moody believed they'd just seen?

A few days later, during his lunch break at the coffee roaster's, Moody, who had an unimportant letter to mail, set out on foot in the direction of the post office. He rounded, or rather squared, the corner into an alley he used as a shortcut and then screamed, or no, he didn't scream, but he wanted to, for there at eye level was a grinning face made of bones—bones with no flesh over them. Moody drew back from it, a hand raised to ward off the thing, which, upon closer inspection, was an ingeniously constructed cube. Six grinning bone faces, each about four inches in diameter, were tied together with wire, and the whole thing was suspended by a thicker wire from a rusty fire escape overhead.

Giving the thing a wide berth, Moody resumed walking. He wondered three things: What kind of bones had been used to make the cube? What was it these days with cubes in public places? And was it an omen?

He hoped it wasn't an omen. If it were—if it was?—it signified either nothing or, more likely, something bad. There was, surely, nothing to be gained by coming unexpectedly face to face with a six-faced hanging sculpture of doom. It occurred to him that the cube had one death-face for each deceased member of his true love's family, if you counted the dog and cat. He shuddered. But of course, any cube at all would have had that same number of faces, so maybe the coincidence wasn't so terrible. His footsteps seemed unnaturally loud in the alleyway. I really must get to work on the improvisation Kate requested, he said to himself. What I need is a deadline.

I need a deadline, he said to Kate that night in the kitchen.

She shrugged. End of the year? she said.

You got it, said Moody.

They were making spaghetti. The year was several months from ending, but already the air outside was cool enough that they'd closed their kitchen windows. Steam from the boiling water condensed on the glass. Moody told Kate about the cube of bones and the fright it had given him. He didn't mention that it had reminded him of her family.

I saw a cube today too, Kate said without looking up from the garlic she was chopping. It wasn't scary, though, she said. It was just a metal cube, nothing special.

Where'd you see it? said Moody.

It was sitting on somebody's lawn, said Kate. I concede that it was probably supposed to be art.

Moody wanted to say, Are you sure it wasn't a metal barn?

Instead he said, Is there any way I can help with dinner?

Grate some cheese, she said.

He did. Then he said, Anything else?

Put on some music, how 'bout, she said.

Moody put on a recording of one of Scriabin's direst pieces, his Black Mass Sonata.

Nice, said Kate.

Yeah, said Moody.

They ate without speaking as the piano chords crashed around them. Sometimes we almost get the feeling that these young lovers knew that one of them was not long for the world.

38

Had you told Amanda a week before the *Faces* performance that cubes were the answer to ennui, she would have said, Whatever.

Had you told her the same thing a week after the event, she would have said, Well, duh.

Here's how it happened.

After seeing Chad's cubes at Gallery Five, Amanda told Ralph she had a headache and wanted to be alone.

But I need you, he said.

Not tonight, she said.

Then she raced home, or, well, she traveled home at a normal speed and began making cubes. She was a fan of a sugary cereal called Puff! Puff!, and the first few cubes she made were made out of Puff! Puff! box panels. These cubes were nothing special, Amanda could see, but they were special to her, for they were the first sculptures she'd made in years. Plus, they were cubes, and cubes were great! Amanda couldn't have said why she fell so immediately in love with the cube form. Maybe it was that the form imposed a degree of order that was lacking in most other things, including life, the world, and society. Or maybe it was simpler than that: maybe she just liked cubes, period.

At one o'clock in the morning on that first night of cubemaking, Amanda stepped onto her rusty fire escape to smoke a cigarette. I really should stop smoking, she thought, and with great relish she took a deep drag, held the smoke in her lungs for a long, blissful moment, and then exhaled luxuriously into the damp night air. It felt so good to be making real art again. No more bullshit performance art for me, Amanda thought, and she hoped she meant it.

She looked in through the window. There they were, the Puff! Puff! cubes. They were all primary colors—much too cheerful for her taste. Seeing them now in the kitchen glow, Amanda couldn't believe they'd come from her. Good cheer wasn't the thing she was destined to contribute to the long sweep of humanity's artistic gropings, she felt. Leave aside the question of whether gropings can sweep. Amanda turned from the window and peered into the dark alley beneath her fire escape. She'd seen some bones down there the other day, and now, moved by a sudden impulse, she flicked her cigarette butt into the night air and went in through the apartment and out the door into the hallway, etc., and soon found herself in the alley at the spot where, sure enough, a small pile of disarranged bones yet sat. She had no idea what sort of animal the bones were the last remaining evidence of. Cat? Possum? Skunk? Shoving aside her concerns about hygiene, Amanda picked up the bones and dropped them into a plastic bag she'd brought with her. She wondered if perhaps the animal, whatever it had been, had caught a glimpse of her face in the window on the brick wall above and been slain by her good looks. Of course, there were other reasons an animal might die.

Amanda took the bag of bones inside, brewed a pot of coffee, and got back to work. By the time dawn rolled around, she had made a six-faced bone cube and hung it by a wire from her fire escape. It was, as you will by now have guessed, bright reader that you are, the very same cube Moody would run into sometime later when he took a shortcut down the alley on his way to the post office.

Do you mind if I come over so we can practice for *Sexploits*? said Ralph the next day on the phone.

I do mind, Ralph, said Amanda. I'm done with that sort of thing.

Uh, hang on, said Ralph. I don't think I heard you right.

You heard me, said Amanda. No more of that shit.

What's gotten into you? he said.

Cubes.

Cubes! said Ralph. I dreamed about them all night. Let's talk.

Fine, said Amanda. Come over.

They had sex on the fire escape while the bone cube swung below them. Later, after a dinner of rice and beans, they began incubating a plan, which soon hatched. It was this: Persuade Chad to join them in a new artistic movement called New Cubism. Chad would be the prophet, they his disciples. It was the only way Amanda could think of that she could legitimately go on making cubes, or at least making them for public consumption. If she made cubes outside any association with Chad, people would say she had stolen his idea. Which, yes, she had, but only because his idea was so freaking good.

I was thinking maybe I could make some cubes too, said Ralph as he piled the dishes in the sink.

Sure, why not, said Amanda, though she knew that it would be hard for a one-dimensional character like Ralph to work in a three-dimensional medium.

A few days later, having arranged to meet Chad at a pub for a round of beers, Amanda and Ralph met Chad at a pub for a round of beers.

What's this about? said Chad, who was none too sure he wanted to be there, though a free pale ale was, as his mother used to say, nothing at which to shake a stick.

Amanda leaned toward him, giving him an unobstructed view of what was inside her V-neck sweater. Her knee touched his under the table, and she looked at him with bedroom eyes.

Ralph said, We think your cubes are brilliant.

I'm gay, said Chad to Amanda.

Oh, she said, withdrawing her knee and sitting up straighter. Sorry.

Chad's other knee now registered the touch of Ralph's below the table.

Please stop that, Chad said, and just tell me why you asked for this meeting.

Ralph's knee retreated as his mouth said, Right. Sorry. Your cubes. Unbelievable. Very moving stuff. Amanda makes cubes too. Even I—

You'd better not try to steal my idea, said Chad.

We want to be your disciples, Amanda said. You are, as you must know, the founder of New Cubism. You are the prophet. We can help you get your vision out into the world. Let's all three of us make a bunch of cubes and deposit them in strategic locations throughout the City. Or perhaps there won't be a strategy. New Cubism is what the City needs right now—one of the things it needs. No other shape affects people the way a cube does. I, for instance, feel alive for the first time in years, and it's all because I've begun making cubes. I owe my new life to you.

If I let you two in on this, said Chad, who in spite of himself was flattered, you're going to want it to be all about sex. It can't just be tit cubes and ass cubes and prick cubes and cubes of copulation.

Ball cubes, said Ralph.

Don't worry, said Amanda, we're done with all that.

Almost done, said Ralph.

Why should I believe that either of you can make a cube worth looking at? said Chad, remembering a theory of the particularity of individual expression he'd read about in one of his arts magazines. Don't expect a painter to make a good sculpture, the magazine had said, or a poet to write a novel with a plot. It followed that a pair of sex-obsessed performance artists might not be able to make an artistically meaningful cube.

Let's take a short walk, said Amanda.

She and Ralph led Chad to the alley by her apartment to see the bone-face cube. Chad was stunned. It was chilling, the thing. He wished he'd thought of it—he'd never have thought of it. He did sad; Amanda did icy.

It's brilliant, said Chad. But what kind of cubes do you make? he said to Ralph.

I don't know yet, said Ralph.

He's more of an idea man, said Amanda. He can come up with a strategy for our movement.

We don't need a strategy, said Chad.

We'll see, said Amanda. So, are you in?

Chad took a deep breath. He started coughing, but that was just because he was unaccustomed to taking deep breaths.

I'm in, he said.

The rest, dear reader, is fictional history.

39

What's wrong? said Dr. Love, aware that it was cold of him to be standing over his wife rather than sitting next to her and putting his arm around her—but he had his suspicions.

Sylvia shook her head, still sobbing, still not meeting his eye.

It had been years since Dr. Love had seen his wife cry—a sure sign of trouble in the marriage, now that he thought about it. He sat down beside her, not too close, and held out a hand, palm up, to see if she would take it. She did. He drew her to him, and she cried a bit on his shoulder.

When she had quieted down, he said, Tell me.

James is leaving, she said, and immediately she began crying again.

At the mention of the name of the man he'd come to regard as his rival for the affections of his wife of twenty-seven years, Dr. Love experienced something like global warming, except it wasn't global, it was just inside him, and it was a cooling instead of a warming. To keep from plummeting toward absolute zero, he reminded himself that even if Sylvia left him, there would still be plenty of bourbon in the world—too much, really—and he could buy his fair share of it and then some, to say nothing of sleeping pills. But this was just one corner of his mind talking. The other seven (yes, a mind, like a cube, has eight corners) were busy searching Sylvia's demeanor for clues.

What do you mean, he's leaving? he said.

He accepted an offer of another job, Sylvia said.

Where? said Dr. Love.

She named a for-profit corporation headquartered two thousand miles to the west of the City—very nearly far enough away, in Dr. Love's opinion.

How much notice did he give? Dr. Love said.

Oh, said Sylvia, drawing away from him and sitting up straighter and once again not exactly meeting his eye. He's staying to finish the annual report. But that's it. After that we're doomed.

You're not doomed, said Dr. Love.

We are, said Sylvia. He's irreplaceable. And! The bastard's going over to the other side.

She meant he was going to do finances for an entity that made a profit. For Sylvia, that was the ultimate betrayal.

His wife's crying had made her prettier, Dr. Love noticed. It had softened her face, which had had, lately, a hard edge to it, at least around him. Even on occasions when she hadn't been crying, she was way out toward the more attractive edge of the bell curve charting the attractiveness or unattractiveness of women her age—something any straight man (but was James straight?) could not have failed to notice.

Dr. Love took a deep breath and said, Is there anything you're not telling me?

She looked at him blankly. What do you mean by that? she said.

Dr. Love was encouraged by the fact that she

hadn't said no. When people were lying, they generally said what they thought they were expected to say. When they were telling the truth, they just said whatever popped into their heads. Of course, it was the other way around in the case of a compulsive liar, but Sylvia wasn't one of those—was she?

I mean, said Dr. Love, that you were sobbing. That's all. Literally sobbing. Which is an extreme reaction to the loss of an employee, no matter how valued that employee is. Which leads me to wonder, not for the first time, if maybe James has been more to you than just an employee. Is all.

There, he thought. I said it.

Sylvia stared at him for a moment and then burst out laughing. She put her hands to her face and laughed as uncontrollably as, a minute earlier, she'd cried. She even toppled away from Dr. Love and curled into a ball of hilarity on the couch.

Oh, Fred, she said when she'd partly regained her composure. You're such an idiot! James doesn't like women. I'm not sure he likes men either. I don't know what his deal is. But, my god, I would sooner sleep with... with a... I don't know, an alien or something.

I would appreciate it if you didn't make fun of me, said Dr. Love.

Fred, Sylvia said, and she turned toward him and put her hands on his shoulders. You are the love of my life.

Affordable housing is the love of your life, said Dr. Love.

No, she said, smiling. You.

Then why are we sleeping in different beds? Dr. Love shouted.

Sylvia recoiled and withdrew her hands.

Because we have different schedules! she shouted. Because we're old! Don't shout at me!

Husband and wife arose and paced the room, he counterclockwise, she also counterclockwise. Then they returned to the couch and sat close together without speaking. Dr. Love thought of the first time they'd sat together on a couch, some twenty-nine and one-half years ago. Their whole lives ahead of them.

After a minute, Sylvia said, Would you like some tea?

Yes, Dr. Love said.

She got up and went to the kitchen and made the sounds that are made when tea is being prepared. She returned with two cups of tea, each of them resting delicately on a thin saucer that trembled slightly in one or the other of her hands, which, on Dr. Love's watch, had changed from those of a young woman to those of a woman who was no longer young.

They sipped their tea in silence. Then Dr. Love opened his arms, and his wife nestled into the circle they made, a circle he then closed around her as though to prevent her escape—but she wasn't trying to escape, he realized.

Let's go to the opera sometime, Dr. Love said. May I take you to the opera?

Oh, hell, yes, Sylvia said.

Dr. Love sighed. He didn't care for the opera,

but he knew how much Sylvia liked it. Anyway, all was well now. All was well.

That night, for the first time in ages, Dr. Love and his wife slept in the same bed.

40

Teach me to play tennis, Kate said to Moody one sunny day in mid-autumn.

Moody raised an eyebrow at her over his cup of strong black coffee. They were sitting at the kitchen table.

You don't have to pretend to be interested in tennis to prove that you love me, he said.

Doofus, said Kate. I want to learn. Besides, I only pretend in bed.

Ha ha, said Moody, though the remark worried him.

He took her to the public courts in the park up the street. The courts were in bad repair, and so was Moody's tennis game, but that didn't matter. He showed Kate how to hold the racket, how to position her feet, how and when to step into the shot. He told her it was important to transfer her weight, slight though it was, through the shot, and to remain at all times on her toes, not her heels.

Swing from low to high, he said. Like this. And remember, the key to the game is anticipation. That and consistency. Though it's important to be aggressive too. But what matters most is footwork. That and clear thinking.

Kate sat down on the court, laughing.

Maybe we should take things a little more slowly, she said.

Moody smiled ruefully. I got a little too excited, maybe, he said.

Maybe, she said.

So they took things more slowly. Moody loved watching Kate try out the unfamiliar movements. He could see her thinking of the things he'd told her and trying to perform the actions individually rather than in one continuous flow—which was only natural for a beginner. She could swing from low to high but not while also transferring her weight into the shot, for instance. None of this mattered, of course. It was a beautiful day, arguably the most beautiful in history. It was suicide-postponement weather. Not only wasn't there a cloud in the sky; there also wasn't, as far as Moody could see, a cloud anywhere on the horizon of his life. His heart swelled with love for this beautiful, strange girl, this girl from a star-crossed family, this girl who for some reason had chosen him as a person to be with, at least for now, when, presumably, she could have chosen someone else.

Out! he said as yet another of Kate's shots failed to land within the court's boundaries.

But close! Kate said.

Yes, close, said Moody, smiling. Now try again.

How happy I am, he thought.

41

A few days later, the country went to war again. This war was even less justifiable than the one he'd protested in college, Moody felt. Kate shared his opinion. So did a few hundred thousand other people who converged, not by chance, on one of the City's main boulevards one chilly Saturday. Moody found it thrilling to be part of so large a group of people who were all disgusted by the same thing. Speeches were made, slogans were chanted, cleverly worded signs were held aloft. A lot of attractive women opposed the war, Moody noticed—same as during the last war—but it didn't matter. The world was ruled by men, not women—not even beautiful women.

The day got colder and colder. At length, Moody and Kate ducked out of the protest and went to a noodle house for lunch. Nothing warms a discouraged peacenik like a big bowl of noodles in broth, as is well known. In the booth across the aisle from theirs sat, unattended by any human, a cube of granite with an etching on its side that read, R.I.P., Peace.

It's nice to know the cubes are on our side, said Moody.

That night, home again, they watched footage of the protest on television. The police had started roughing people up, apparently, and had arrested several hundred protesters, sometime after Moody and Kate had gone for lunch. Now the country's leader, who'd started the war without ever clearly explaining why, appeared on the screen to deliver an address to the nation. He thanked the protesters for making their opinions known.

You have been heard, he said. That's what's so great about this country. Everyone gets to say whatever they want. However, in this case, I don't agree with what you said. And a lot of other people don't either. So now would be a good time to go back to your small, private lives and not worry so much about what's happening on the other side of the world, okay? I'll take care of that stuff. You all just mind your own business. Thank you, and god bless.

Unbelievable, said Moody.

What an asshole, Kate said.

They switched off the TV and began a game of Scrabble. Moody, who kept drawing tiles with vowels on them—useful tiles, but only if you didn't have too many of them—felt that he'd been wronged, personally wronged, not by the Scrabble tiles but by his country, or history, or whatever. From everything he'd ever read about it, war really was hell. How could it be entered into so lightly?

Bingo, said Kate.

That was what a player said when she was able to play all her tiles in one turn. This was bad news for the other player or players.

Goddamn, said Moody as Kate laid her tiles across the board.

Take that! said Kate.

No, I mean, I was just thinking, said Moody.

Kate's forehead bunched as she tallied her points.

We're doing exactly what our brave leader wants us to do, said Moody.

Playing Scrabble? she said.

Minding our own business, Moody said. Living our little lives.

Oh, said Kate. Yeah. Well, I just scored seventy-two points.

The world is so depressing, said Moody.

You just figured that out? said Kate.

Moody blinked.

Cheer up, said Kate. The world is no more horrible now than it was at any other point in history.

But shouldn't it be getting better? said Moody. Two steps forward, one step back?

Kate shrugged and said, Who knows? Maybe that is what is happening. Anyway, it's your turn.

I can't possibly win, said Moody, eyeing his letters.

That may be, said Kate, but you're obligated to play the game to the end.

42

Sylvia was among the protesters who were arrested. She wasn't a big antiwar person in general, but she'd attended the protest as a favor to her friend Louise, who'd often accompanied her to demonstrations on behalf of affordable housing. Louise was arrested too, and, worse luck, her shoulder was slightly dislocated when a policeman yanked on her arm, which was in late middle age. The two women were ushered into a police van with a dozen other protesters and driven to the justice system's nearest intake center, where they were held for six hours before being fingerprinted, photographed, and entered into the police department's permanent database of persons on whom to keep an eye. What crime are we accused of? Louise kept saying, but the man handling their case said nothing. He was pulling an overtime shift and was out of sleep, hadn't had enough coffee, and nursed a dark intuition that he might soon die of testicular cancer, even though he'd received no such diagnosis. He resented these self-righteous rabble rousers for having cost him a day at home with his wife and kids—the more so as he feared his days were numbered.

Of course, everyone's days are numbered. Most people don't know the number, is all.

That's where we come in.

Chad at this point had 10,958 days to live. That's thirty years and a day, accounting for leap years. He would have plenty of time, in other words, to enjoy the runaway success of the artistic movement he'd accidentally founded. It was the perfect kind of success, in his opinion. Never fully welcomed by the City's art establishment, the New Cubists and their new cubes were enthusiastically and often literally embraced by the City's people. To happen upon an unlooked-for cube in a public space became a rite of passage for native-born City dwellers and a mark of distinction for transplants from other locales who hoped to, quote, make it in the City. Chad became a kind of anticelebrity and slept alone less often than he had before. Of course, none of these successes led Chad to stop being sad. To be Chad was to be sad, and to be sad was, at least in his case, to be Chad. But that was okay, as Chad had learned with the help of Dr. Love. To be who you were was the whole point of being who you were.

Things didn't go nearly so well for Ralph. He was to live only another 411 days before, according to police reports, he fell or jumped from Amanda's rusty fire escape into the waiting arms of a truly bone-crushing demise. His death would break the heart of his father, an auto mechanic named Jim who would forever reproach himself for not having shown his son more warmth when he was growing up. He would press a permanently greasy hand to his head and say, It's my fault he went away and got mixed up with those people, by which he meant artists. He knew his wife agreed that it was his fault, though she didn't say so.

Amanda's number was a hefty 25,132. She soon acquired a reputation as the darkest and most original of the New Cubists. Though she made far fewer cubes than did Chad or the more energetic of their apprentices, her cubes never failed to cause a stir. An invisible cube that she claimed represented love sparked no end of controversy. My kid could've made that, some people quipped. Others dug deeper: Did the artist mean to suggest that there was no such thing as love? Or that love was indeed right under our noses but we had to take it on faith? Or, more narrowly and poignantly, was Amanda simply bemoaning the absence of lasting love from her own life? She didn't give interviews, so it was left to the viewer to decide how, and whether, to answer such questions.

Amanda enjoyed the initial stages of time's erosion of her unparalleled beauty. It was a relief to know, as each successive day crashed to an end, that she was a little bit less lethal than she'd been at the close of the day before. The waxing of her unasked-for powers in her late teens and through her twenties had been very traumatic for her, not just for others. (She peaked on her thirtieth birthday; the party was a massacre.) She hated her looks as much as she loved and needed them. In other words, she felt about her appearance the way a lot of other people felt about it. The whole dynamic was tiresome and unoriginal, yet it was still a shock when, in her late forties, she began hearing remarks from passersby like *Such an attractive older woman*. The condescension of this turn of phrase filled her with a desire she was already full of anyway: the desire to be free of human society. One day at dawn she resolved never again to speak. That did the trick. Her few friends drifted away, and she spent the final decades of her long life in a tiny tenth-floor apartment, making the occasional cube, studying the play of light and shadow across the City's rooftops, drinking green tea, and so on. She was neither happy nor unhappy.

At least I know I'm alive, she would say silently to herself.

Radicalized by her arrest and the dislocation of her friend's shoulder, Sylvia devoted her remaining 6,972 days to editing an antiwar magazine she and Louise founded. It was called *Let's All Stand Back and Let Death Happen Naturally*, and although its effect on the course of world history cannot be precisely quantified, most estimates place the number in the vicinity of zero. So much for her days. Most of her remaining 6,972 evenings Sylvia allocated to the physical and emotional maintenance of Dr. Love, who may have been good at helping other people help themselves but was not good at helping himself. The man couldn't cook a pot of spaghetti.

At night, Sylvia and Dr. Love went to bed, often together, sometimes apart, never with any third party.

To Dr. Love were given, in addition to all that had been given already, 6,602 days and as many nights. He got his beach-house retirement. Many were the hours he spent in his rocking recliner on the porch, glass of bourbon and/or pipe of tobacco in hand, loafers on feet, newspaper within reach, wife within earshot. Many too were the walks he took up and down the beach, the last of which coincided with the arrival onshore of a rogue wave that was so large as to be a rogue among rogues—a real rogue wave's rogue wave. Dr. Love was pulled out to sea along with a few other unfortunates. He treaded water for a minute or two, but he was not a strong swimmer. Even as he sank, nay, even as he took in that first awful lungful of water (which soothed somewhat the discomfort of the nascent emphysema with which he was never to have the opportunity to become terminally ill), Dr. Love caught a glimpse of an almost grotesquely beautiful tropical fish that had been swept along for hundreds of miles by the rogue wave. His last thought was not, as might have been expected, the song lyric *Knowing that you'll think of me and cry*. Rather, it was: I wish Sylvia could have seen that fish.

Kate has been appointed to outlive everyone else in this book, including the police functionary who did indeed have cancer of the balls and would live only another 235 days—a rotten fate, but at least the man was spared knowing that his wife would be so much happier in her second marriage. Not that he would have wished her unhappiness. It's a complicated business, this taking leave of one's nearest and dearest who burst yet with life. But we digress.

To Kate were yet allotted an astonishing 29,444 mornings, nights, afternoons, you name it.

It was a future large enough to crush a weaker person. But Kate was strong by nature and had been made stronger by the losses she'd suffered. Soon, with his family's permission and in their weepy company, she, dry-eyed, will scatter Moody's ashes from the very point of land about which he will in the nick of time have written the definitive musical composition/improvisation. (More on that shortly.) After that sad day, Kate will retreat for a while into her work at the stationery shop and into the novels about nineteenth-century sea disasters she'll read at night to help herself sleep. Before long, though—for life has a way of going on—she'll be haunting anew the cheese tables of the City's art galleries, looking for a new mate. Indeed, she'll find one and marry him: Chad.

Ha! Just kidding. Kate will never marry. Moody had been the fellow for her, and she knew it. It was too bad, since he went and died on her, just like everyone else she ever really cared about. At length, Kate will give up on love and become a scholar. She'll pass the years situating narratives in the context of other narratives, arguments in the context of other arguments, despair in the context of other responses to the human predicament. Dreary work, but it will help her pass the time. So will bike riding.

Enough. We have one more piece of business to attend to before we dismiss our protagonist, who has but two days to live.

43

Moody, hi. Thanks for dropping by.

Where am I?

We've pulled you outside the story for a moment, Moody. Please take a seat. This is your exit interview.

I'm—being fired?

In a sense, yes.

From the coffee roaster's?

From that and everything else.

You don't mean...?!

We do mean. Finger across neck. Your time's almost up, son.

But I'm in love!

You and a billion other people. Do you think that makes you special?

I guess not.

Oho, wrong again. Not everyone gets to find love before they die, Moody. Some people—

—don't even get to look. I know.

We're glad you're able to be philosophical about this. It's one of the things we like about how we made you.

Sorry, but what kind of novel is this? Shouldn't I have to make some kind of big defining choice or screw something up and then try to fix it?

Not all novels are cut from the same cloth, Moody. Strictly speaking, your much-touted moodiness is the Chekhovian gun that ought to have been fired but hasn't been. But remember, this is only secondarily a novel. Primarily it's your life, and life has a way of not being art.

What kind of gun?

Never mind. The point is, it's over. Everyone's life is like that. Everyone thinks a lot of things are going to happen, but then only some of them do. Do you want us to leave you alone for a minute to come to terms with this? Before we do the interview?

I... But I...

Don't cry, son. This happens to everyone. Be strong.

Oh, god... Okay... I guess now at least I don't have to choose a career.

That's the spirit! And at the eleventh hour he reveals he has a sense of humor. Excellent. Now, here's what's going to happen. You've a little time to live yet, and before you leave this office, we'll dab a bit of ointment behind your ears that will make you forget everything that's been said here. You won't spend your remaining hours screaming in terror. You'll be left with just a vague sense of foreboding, a feeling of urgency that will help you do whatever matters most to you during what remains of your time on earth. Every mortal should be so lucky.

Gee, thanks.

Don't mention it. Now, Moody, we want you to know, first of all, that we're not letting you go because of any displeasure on our part with how you've performed your duties as protagonist.

Tell the truth.

We mean it. You're a nice guy, you have feelings, you occasionally do stuff. Maybe you could have been a little more active, had fewer thoughts, etc., but all in all, you've done the job we asked you to do, and we thank you.

I don't remember being asked—

We do think you should have tried to sleep with Amanda one time, just for the hell of it, but we understand that you're not a plucker of fruit. You're an eater of the fruits that fall in your lap, as it were, or at your feet or even on your head. That's okay. We made you that way. We're not complaining.

It sounds as if you are.

Eh, just a little. Now. The big question we have for you is, Do you feel you've learned anything about love?

From you? No.

Not from us. From your life, the story of your life. Please take this seriously, Moody. You won't get another crack at these questions.

Sorry. Okay. Love, you say? Well, yeah. I really love Kate, for starters. I can't believe she wants to be with me. And I love my family.

More generally, though? Anything about the nature of love?

It's something you go out and look for in the world, I think, but it's really mostly inside you, is what I would say if pressed.

Not bad, kid. A little trite, but most truths are. Anything else?

No.

Moving on. Is there anything you would

change about the narrative of your life if you could?

The things that happened or the way you guys told them?

Either one.

I guess I wouldn't have minded living a bit longer.

Naturally.

And why did you have to kill Kate's entire family? That's pretty messed up. Do you realize what it's done to her?

Better than you do, Moody. And we didn't kill them. They just died, and we told how it happened. That's all.

Why should I believe you? I don't know what powers you have. I don't even know who you are.

Yeah, we're not going to go into that. You're free to go now.

That's it?

Yes.

May I ask you some questions first?

We'll give you four. No, three.

Will I see my mother again?

No.

My father or brothers?

You're pissing away your questions here, Moody. Be smart about how you phrase things. But no, you won't see them again. Last question.

Jesus. All right. Give me a second.

Tick. Tick.

Don't do that!

Tick.

Okay. Will you do something for me? One

little thing?

Depends.

Will you do whatever you can to make this as easy for Kate as it can possibly be?

It's not going to be easy for her.

I know, but will you do something? Anything at all? Don't let her be the one to find my mangled body, at least.

You got it.

It would be nice if I didn't get mangled, actually.

Time's up. Turn your head so we can apply the ointment.

Can I say one more thing?

Lord, you are a talker once you get going.

I just want to say I—I guess I've enjoyed working here.

No, you haven't, Moody, but it's nice of you to say. Now let us see those ears.

44

Moody jabbed at the alarm clock and snuggled closer to Kate to sleep for another fifteen minutes, the way he did every morning. This morning, however, he was gripped by an anxiety whose source he couldn't pinpoint. He couldn't go back to sleep, couldn't even keep his eyes closed, and so he got up and started the coffee pot going and got into the shower. While he was rinsing the shampoo from his hair, he realized why he was anxious: he'd been dithering far too long about finishing the composition/improvisation Kate had requested of him. He felt guilty about it, though also very slightly resentful that she had the power to make him feel guilty—except no, she wasn't making him feel guilty, he was making himself feel guilty. Whatever the case, he wanted to please her, and so after work that night he called to say he wouldn't be home for dinner because he was going to the church to play the piano for an hour or two.

I'll leave out a plate of food for you, said Kate. Remember, tonight's the night I play cards with Ginny and Alex.

I won't wait up, Moody said. Kick their asses.

I always do, she said.

Moody'd been having all sorts of trouble hitting upon a musical theme that would capture the way he imagined Kate must feel about that rocky point of land. Tonight, on his way to the church, he realized he'd been approaching the task all wrong.

He should focus on how he felt about the place, not how he thought she might feel. The music had to come from him, after all; he couldn't somehow get it to come from her. And Moody didn't feel the point of land was gloomy—he thought it was beautiful, beautiful in its honesty, its lack of pretension or ornament. Admittedly, he'd seen it only once, and on a sunny day, but as that was all he had to go by, go by it he would.

At the piano, Moody started playing something in C major, the most forthright of all keys. And now an interesting thing happened: his feelings about the place's beauty became entwined with the sense of anxiety he'd awoken with that morning and never quite shaken all day. These twin emotions propelled him into an improvisational mode that somehow captured both the crisp sunshine he'd seen falling upon the rocks (that was the C major) and the angst he knew Kate felt about the place where she'd scattered the ashes of just about everyone she'd ever loved (he switched to F minor). And just like that, the composition/improvisation assembled itself.

It was Moody's finest hour as a composer and one of his five or six finest hours as an improviser.

The next night, he took Kate with him to the church.

The janitor let them in and said, God loves you.

Thank him for us, said Moody.

This was a little running joke they had. It didn't run very far—that was the whole thing.

Kate looked extra good to Moody tonight for some reason. Maybe it was the way the barrette held her hair, or maybe it was the checkered skirt she wore over black tights over those legs he knew and really, really liked, or maybe it was the top half of her outfit, which was also just right, or maybe there was just something exciting about being alone with the woman he loved in the dimly lighted basement of a church. Whatever the reason, he had a strong urge to ravish her then and there. But the janitor might reappear at any moment, and so instead of ravishing the love of his life, Moody gave her a chaste squeeze and sat her down next to him on the piano bench.

He opened confidently with the C major theme, the one about the honest sunlight falling unpretentiously on the strong rocks, and then he began working in the F minor theme with its overtones of death and loss and grief and unanswerable questions. He played with feeling but didn't overdo it, and he developed each theme to its fullest extent but no further. There was a maturity to his playing that hadn't always been there, for instance when he was younger and less mature. When he finished, he turned to Kate to find her eyes shining, perhaps with tears, perhaps with love, perhaps with some unrelated thought she was having.

It's perfect, she said.

They kissed a bit, and then Moody said, Let's go get a drink.

They sat close together in a booth in the back room of the bar. Moody kept sliding his hand up her thigh, and Kate repeatedly nudged it back down, but with less conviction each time. What did it matter? There was no one else in the room. They hadn't even finished their drinks when Moody, whose temperature had been steadily rising, pulled Kate by the hand out of the booth and out the back door of the bar and up the street to the door next to the cheese shop, which was the door to the stairs that led to their home. He let go her hand for a moment to deal with the lock on the door. Then, hand in hand once more, they pounded up the steps to the second floor. Again a pause for key and lock. Then into the apartment like a gale-force wind.

The storm of their lovemaking began on one of the kitchen chairs, Kate astride Moody, Moody on the chair, the chair upon the worn linoleum floor that was above the first-floor ceiling that was above the air in the rooms of the cheese shop, below whose floor was a basement, and so on down through the water table and various layers of rock or whatever until one got to the molten core of the earth, which was really, really hot. After a bit of this, Moody carried Kate into the bedroom and more or less flung her onto the bed, and a moment later they were conjoined once more.

Ah! she said.

Oh! said Moody.

Together they traveled to a world more beautiful than the one Moody was soon to depart. When they returned, they lay in each other's arms until, still half-clothed and with a total of three shoes on, they fell asleep and did not wake until dawn.

45

Dawn. Moody brought his fist down on the alarm clock, almost knocking it off the table by the bed. He curled around Kate for another fifteen minutes of oblivion, which passed in an instant. Again the alarm.

Grrrr, said Moody.

He got up, groggily set about making coffee, and discovered that they were out of coffee filters.

Jesus goddamn motherfucking sonofabitch, he said.

Having fallen asleep the night before with most of the previous day's clothes on, he was dressed again in no time. He bent and kissed a still-sleeping Kate on the ear.

I'm going across the street for coffee filters, he said.

Mmm, said Kate, stirring slightly but not waking.

Kate liked to sleep face down, her arms crossed at the wrist just under her chin. Looking at her now, Moody was struck again by how small she was, how fine-boned, how delicate.

I'll always take care of you, he whispered. Then he turned and left.

He yawned as he clomped down the stairs to the street. Kate's sleepy *Mmm* echoed in his mind's ear. He would climb back under the covers with her for just five minutes, he promised himself, after he got the coffee brewing. He smiled at the thought.

Out the door he went and up to the end of the block. Morning traffic whizzed by. Moody waited at the corner for the light to change—and was jolted more fully awake than he'd yet been today, not that that was saying much, by the sight of a very beautiful woman waiting across the street for the same light. She was no Amanda, but she was close. Just an absolutely perfect body, and she knew it, you could tell by the way she stood and by the amused half-smile that played at the corners of her mouth. She was dressed in that year's fashion for girls who were into rock and roll, though hers was a modified version of the outfit (a sweater instead of a T-shirt with holes in it) that suggested she was on her way to work and not, as Moody might have preferred to fantasize (not that he was even awake enough to have such complicated thoughts), heading home from an all-night party. Her dark jeans were, if anything, tighter than the skin they enclosed.

The light turned green.

Moody, who was about to go to the grave a shy man, dared meet the woman's eye only fleetingly as their paths crossed at the midpoint of the crosswalk. Or rather, his eye fell briefly upon hers; she amusedly refused to meet his gaze or anyone else's.

A man who is shy is yet a man, however. And what is a man? A man is an awkward hybrid of a human being and a dog. No sooner did the woman pass him in the crosswalk than Moody—even though coffee filters and crawling back into bed with his true love were foremost in his mind—

turned and, while still walking across the street, stared for a moment back over his left shoulder at the woman's ass, which, though it had its equals no doubt, was not likely ever to be surpassed.

Had the woman passed to his right instead of his left, Moody would have glanced not over his left shoulder but over his right. If only that had been the case, Moody would surely have seen the speeding car whose driver, instead of braking, was staring at the same thing that commanded Moody's attention. Even if Moody had been able to ingest just a drop or two of coffee before leaving home, we believe, he would have been alert enough to sense the car's approach no matter where he was looking. That's why we made sure he and Kate were out of coffee filters. We knew Moody pretty well, after all, well enough to be certain that without coffee he was, on this even more than on other mornings, as good as dead.

Kate, whom we've blessed with not only the strength of character required to persevere in the wake of yet another devastating loss but also the ability to sleep through almost anything, did not wake at the noise of the accident outside her window and so was spared the worst of the sights to be seen that day.

46

As for Moody: Yes, he was dead now, but consider that unlike many millions of others, he got to not only: a) look for love and even b) find it but also c) die before he lost, to another man or time's steady erosion or some other cause or force, the love that he'd found.

In other words, Moody got to go out on a high note. Everyone should be so lucky.

Acknowledgments

Thanks to Samantha Shea and Anne Borchardt and everyone else at Georges Borchardt Inc. for their unswerving belief in this book. Thanks to Jon Roemer for publishing it and making it look so beautiful. Thanks to Christine Schutt, John Casey, and other folks at the Sewanee Writers' Conference, as well as the members of the Greenpoint Writers Group, for their helpful comments on earlier drafts. Thanks also to my good friends Bart Skarzynski, Kyle Minor, and Maureen Traverse. A special thanks to the good folks at *One Story* magazine and BOA Editions. Also, thanks to lots of other people for being great! Most of all, thanks to my father, my brothers and their families, my dear late mother, and my excellent wife. This is, after all, a book about love.

About the Author

Douglas Watson's first book, *The Era of Not Quite*, won the inaugural BOA Editions Short Fiction Prize and was published in 2013. His stories have appeared in *One Story*, *Ecotone*, and other publications. *A Moody Fellow Finds Love and Then Dies* is his first novel. He lives in New York City with his wife, the poet Michelle Y. Burke.

CPSI/
Printe
LVOV

415